GORDON KORMAN

BOOK ONE: THE DISCOVERY

DIVE

SO-AHB-975

AN
APPLE
PAPERBACK

SCHOLASTIC INC.
New York Toronto London Auckland Sydney
Mexico City New Delhi Hong Kong Buenos Aires

For Ron Kurtz,
Bubble Blower Extraordinaire

ISBN 0-439-50722-7

Copyright © 2003 by Gordon Korman.
All rights reserved. Published by Scholastic Inc.
SCHOLASTIC and associated logos are trademarks and/or registered trademarks of Scholastic Inc.

12 11   5 6 7 8/0

Printed in the U.S.A.   40

First printing, June 2003

08 September 1665

When the explosion rocked the Griffin, *young Samuel Higgins knew instantly that the boat was doomed.*

Thirteen years old, and dead already, *the ship's boy thought to himself as the towering mainmast splintered in a shower of sparks.*

The sail, now a billowing sheet of flame, settled down over the treasure that lay stacked about on the deck of the barque. Chests piled high with coins and jewels, silver bars by the hundredweight, ropes of pearls, chains of gold. Samuel watched it disappear beneath the burning canvas. He could feel the deck heaving under his feet as the Griffin *began to break apart. A flood of gleaming pieces of eight poured through the gaping holes between the deck planks. It was more money than Samuel had ever seen, worth more, probably, than his entire village in the north of England, and perhaps the surrounding shire as well. It was a fortune that would have turned the head of the king himself.*

THE DISCOVERY

2

And yet it could not buy five more minutes of life for the *Griffin* and her doomed captain and crew.

The voyage back to England would have taken at least three months. The descent to the bottom of the Caribbean took less than three minutes.

There lay the treasure, the spoils of a new world, silent, waiting. . . .

CHAPTER ONE

The catamaran bobbed like a cork, even in the sheltered waters of the harbor on the Caribbean island of Martinique.

Kaz looked dubiously from the flimsy double-hulled boat to the young man who stood balanced on deck, holding out his hand to help the newcomer aboard. "If you want to kill me, why don't you just shoot?"

It got a big laugh. "Come on, Kaczinski. Safest thing afloat."

Swallowing hard, Kaz stepped onto the swaying craft. Putting aside unease was second nature to hockey players, especially in Canada, home of the best of the best. Some of the kids he skated against would go on to NHL careers. They said he'd be one of them — Bobby Kaczinski, the best young defenseman to come out of the Toronto area in the past twenty years.

All that was over now. He stumbled, his knees weak for a moment. It had nothing to do with the motion of the catamaran.

He had come to call it "the dream," although it plagued him as often waking as sleeping.

THE DISCOVERY

Game six of the Ontario Minor Hockey Association finals. Drew Christiansen — Kaz had not known the boy's name then. Now he would never forget it.

Drew Christiansen, whose life he had ruined.

Drew had taken a pass in front of the Red Wings' net. He was Kaz's man, his responsibility. The check was completely legal, clean as a whistle. Everyone agreed on that — the refs, the league officials, even Drew himself. A freak accident, the doctors called it. A one in a million shot.

Kaz remembered the split-second play down to the slightest detail — the urgency to defend his goalie, the satisfaction of a heavy hit. And then a discordant note: *He's not getting up.* And then, *Why is his neck at that funny angle?*

Followed by the nightmare truth: Drew Christiansen would never walk again.

The handshake of greeting came just in time to steady Kaz.

"Tad Cutter, Poseidon Oceanographic Institute," the young man introduced himself. "I'm leading your dive team."

"People call me Kaz." He tried to size up the institute man. Mostly, he was searching for some hint as to why a world-famous oceanographic group had selected a beginning diver for a summer internship. A month ago, Kaz had never stepped into flippers in his life. It had been a mad scramble to get scuba-certified for this program.

But there were no clues in Cutter's blond, blue-eyed features. He flashed white teeth. "Sit tight and start on your tan, okay? I've got one more to pick up." He leaped onto the dock and jogged off.

Who am I kidding? Kaz thought. *Poseidon didn't pick me for my diving. Allagash got me this gig.*

Steven P. Allagash was the sports agent Mr. Kaczinski had hired to guide his son's career all the way to the pros. *Ex-agent*, Kaz reminded himself, since Bobby Kaczinski would not be strapping on skates again.

Allagash had been clearly alarmed at the possibility of such a hot prospect getting away. "Don't make any rash decisions," he had urged. "Forget about hockey for a while. Take some time off this summer. Do something you always wanted to do. I'll set the whole thing up. Just name it."

Kaz had drawn a blank. As long as he could remember, his entire life had been hockey. Camps all summer, games and practices all winter. He had never played any other sport. Why risk an injury that could take him out of hockey? He'd never even had a hobby.

"Come on," Allagash had prodded. "What are your interests?"

The entire back wall of the agent's office was an enormous Plexiglas fish tank. Kaz had always been fascinated by the dozens of brightly colored tropical species that moved through the artificial habitat.

"Fish," Kaz had replied finally. "I like fish."

Fish would do. Diving would do. Anything but hockey.

As he dropped his gear and seated himself on the boat, he realized for the first time that he was not alone. Fast asleep amid a mountain of luggage lay another boy, smaller than Kaz, but probably the same age.

The catamaran bumped up against the tires that lined the dock, and the sleeper shook awake.

He rubbed his eyes behind thick glasses and yawned. "You don't look like Adriana, so I guess you must be Bobby."

"Call me Kaz." He indicated the many bags and cases that littered the deck around the other boy. "Diving equipment?"

"Camera equipment. Dante Lewis. I'm a photographer."

"An underwater photographer, right?" Kaz prompted.

Dante shrugged. "That's what we're here to find out."

Kaz was amazed. "Are you telling me that you're new at this too?"

Dante stared at him. "Are *you*?"

"I got certified, like, ten minutes ago!"

Dante was wide-eyed. "I figured they only took me because they needed a photographer. What about you? Any special skills?"

Kaz searched his mind and came up empty. "I used to be a hockey player."

Dante took in the heat shimmer over the endless turquoise Caribbean. "I don't think the rink freezes hard enough down here."

"That's okay," Kaz deadpanned. "I didn't bring my skates." He frowned into the colorful sails in the harbor around them. Poseidon was one of the top ocean research outfits in the world. Renowned scientists begged to get hired on. Fellowships went to graduate students who were proven geniuses. When they threw open four summer internships for kids under sixteen, they must have gotten thousands of applications. Maybe tens of thousands. They had their pick of the universe.

Why choose us? It didn't make any sense.

They'd been waiting for half an hour when Cutter returned with the third team member. Adriana Ballantyne was a tall, slender thirteen-year-old girl who was dressed more for the deck of a

THE DISCOVERY

luxury liner than a weathered island-hopping catamaran that smelled of diesel and fish.

Kaz had never seen anyone so color-coordinated. Her deck shoes matched her belt, the temples of her designer sunglasses, and the leather handles of her luggage.

"Diver, right?" he asked as she stepped aboard.

"Right," she confirmed. "I guess." And even less certainly, "Sort of. I did some scuba in the south of France this past Easter."

What was going on here?

The catamaran may not have been the most elegant craft in the seven seas, but it got the job done. They covered the distance from Martinique to Saint-Luc in two hours. As they rounded the curve of the shoreline, Cutter damped down the engine to slow their speed.

"Hey," he called in the comparative quiet that followed. "There's Star. She's on our team too. Look at her go!"

Three pairs of eyes focused on the clear blue water a couple of hundred yards out from an isolated cove. Star Ling was diving in just mask and snorkel, moving with a strength and expertise that was obvious to any observer. She cruised just below the surface with the pointed, unerring trajectory of a torpedo. When she dove, her descent was crisp and quick, easily conquering her body's natural buoyancy. She sounded deep, unhurried by the need for her next breath — a sign of superior lung capacity.

"She's awesome!" breathed Adriana.

As the catamaran angled in toward the harbor half a mile up the coast, Star took to the surface and swam in to the beach. They watched her rise and step out of the water and onto the sand.

At first, Kaz thought she'd stumbled. But then it happened again. And again.

"She's limping!" he exclaimed out loud. "She's a — " He was about to say "cripple" when the image of Drew Christiansen cut into his mind like a jagged fork of lightning. *You can't use that word*, Kaz thought to himself. *You've forfeited the right*.

"She's handicapped!" Dante exclaimed in wonder.

Cutter laughed. "Don't let her hear you say that! She's the toughest kid I've ever met."

Three beginners and now this, Kaz reflected.

Who was making the decisions at Poseidon Oceanographic?

THE DISCOVERY

CHAPTER TWO

Dr. Geoffrey Gallagher raised his pointer to the bleached skeleton mounted on the wall beside his desk — the gaping jaws of a great white shark, measuring three feet across.

"We see that the teeth are serrated," Poseidon's director lectured to the red light of the video camera that was trained on him, "and angled distinctly inward so that each bite directs the prey down the gullet. *Carcharodon carcharias* has been called nature's perfect predator, the apex of the ocean's food chain. And from personal experience, I can attest to that fact." He tapped a razor-sharp tooth.

With a crack like a rifle shot, the upper jaw fell shut to the lower, snapping the pointer cleanly in two.

Dr. Gallagher jumped back with a very unmacho shriek.

"Cut!" roared the cameraman, doubled over with laughter.

There was a knock at the door.

"Later," called Gallagher, fumbling around for another pointer.

DIVE

The knock came again, this time louder and more insistent.

"Not now!"

The door opened, and in marched Bobby Kaczinski, Dante Lewis, Adriana Ballantyne, and Star Ling.

At first, Gallagher had absolutely no idea who the four teenagers were. Saint-Luc was not a major tourist island like Martinique or Aruba, so the only kids around were locals. Then he remembered the summer internships.

Oh. *Those* kids. He had begged the head office in San Diego to place them somewhere else. But no. It had to be here. Poseidon had even sent a team from California to run the program — Tad Cutter and his crew.

"Welcome!" he beamed, hiding the broken pointer pieces under some papers on his desk. "This is going to be a very exciting summer for you young people. I'm sure you'll be participating in a lot of important research."

They waited, as if for more detail. He stared at them, willing them to go away.

Finally, Star stepped forward. "But Dr. Gallagher, what do we do?"

"Poseidon Saint-Luc is a tremendously busy place," Gallagher explained, "with dozens of different projects all going on at the same time — "

"I mean *now*," she persisted. "What do we do today?"

Gallagher was taken aback. "Well, what does Mr. Cutter say?"

"We haven't seen him since yesterday," supplied Kaz.

"Since *yesterday?*" The director was completely mystified.

The silent man in the room, gray haired and stocky, had been lounging on the couch, observing the videotaping with some amusement. Braden Vanover was one of several ship's captains who worked for Poseidon. He spoke up now. "Cutter and his crew went out at first light on Bill Hamilton's boat."

The director's voice was shrill with frustration. "Why didn't they take these kids? That's the whole reason Cutter's people are here! Without the kids, what are they doing — sunbathing . . . ?" He spied the videographer watching with interest, and fell silent. Jacques Cousteau never had a tantrum when the camera was on him.

Captain Vanover stood up. He had no official connection with the internship program, but he felt bad for the four teens. It was fairly obvious Cutter was ignoring them. "Tell you what. I'll grab English and take them out to get their feet wet."

Gallagher looked pathetically grateful. "Great, great! Did you kids hear that? You're diving today." He put his arm around the shoulders of the girl with the limp. "And I'm sure you'll make an excellent tender while the others are in the water."

Star's eyes flashed. It was obvious to everyone in the room except the director that he had said very much the wrong thing. She was about to speak, was already opening her mouth, when Kaz jumped into the fray.

"Star's a diver like us, Dr. Gallagher," he said quickly. "In fact, she's the best we've got."

"Yes, of course," Gallagher mumbled, and busied himself with resetting the upper portion of the great white's jaw. He very nearly sacrificed a finger as the thing slammed shut again.

It was on the gravel path that led to the guest cabins that Star turned on the big hockey player.

"Where do you get off fighting my battles for me?" she demanded. "When I've got something to say, I say it myself!"

"Yeah, well, maybe that's the problem," Kaz retorted. "If you called Gallagher an idiot — which he is, by the way, so you would have been A-one right — you could have gotten the head of the whole institute mad at us. I wasn't protecting you; I was protecting *me*."

"Even so," she muttered, "mind your own business."

"Count on it," he assured her.

"Hey," said Dante. "We're getting a chance to do something. Let's not blow it."

CHAPTER THREE

Star sat on the deck of the R/V *Hernando Cortés*, watching the harbor at Côte Saint-Luc disappear in the glare of an overpowering Caribbean sun.

"The reefs northeast of the island are pretty spectacular," called Captain Vanover from the cockpit. "They're part of the Hidden Shoals of the French West Indies. Best diving in the world."

Star felt a shiver of excitement. "I know!" she exclaimed. Not from personal experience. But before this trip, she had read everything she could get her hands on about the coral formations around Saint-Luc. This was a great opportunity and she was going to make the most of it.

Kaz, Dante, and Adriana were already struggling into lightweight tropical wet suits. And struggling was the word for it. They looked like three fat ladies trying to squeeze themselves into undersized girdles. Were these guys divers or circus clowns?

Star could slip into a wet suit as easily as putting on a glove. It was a three-second job for her, bad leg and all. Her secret: liquid dish detergent to lubricate her skin. The thin rubber material slid right on.

She made a face, still smarting over Dr. Gallagher's assumption that she couldn't possibly be a diver. People were such idiots about handicaps. They stared at you, pitied you, tried to smooth the way for you. For Star Ling, that limp was normalcy. A mild case of cerebral palsy, that was all — a certain amount of weakness on the left side. She couldn't remember, of course, but her very first step had demonstrated that limp. It was a part of her and always had been.

It wasn't nothing. She didn't delude herself about that. She wouldn't win any footraces or dance with the Bolshoi. But in the water, everything changed. There was no weakness, no asymmetry. She had felt that on her first trip to the county pool, age four. And she still felt it every time she slipped off the dive platform of a boat. The laws of physics that held her back on dry land melted away in a rush of familiarity and comfort that seemed to say, "You're home."

Her eyes wandered aft, where Captain Vanover's lone crew member was hefting heavy scuba tanks as if they weighed nothing. Menasce Gérard was a hulking six-foot-five-inch native dive guide who went by the puzzling nickname "English." No one seemed less English than English, a young West Indian man whose first language was French. Secretly, Star had assigned him a different moniker — Mr. Personality. The guy was just about the most humorless human being she'd ever encountered.

They'd been on the boat for nearly half an hour, and he had yet to crack a smile. In fact, she wasn't sure she could confirm that he had teeth, since he rarely opened his mouth at all. He answered most questions with a series of gestures, shrugs, and grunts.

That didn't stop Adriana from spewing a line of chitchat at him. Maybe that was how things worked at whatever snooty country club her family belonged to. You kept talking without bothering to notice that you weren't getting any answers.

"But why do they call you English?" Adriana burbled on. "You're French, right? I mean, people from Saint-Luc are French citizens."

English barely shrugged as he checked the pressure gauges on the cylinders of compressed air.

"Your name isn't English," she continued. "I just don't understand why anyone would want to call you that."

"Will you give it a rest?" Star groaned. "I once knew a guy named Four Eyes who didn't wear glasses. So they call him English. What's it to you?"

Adriana wasn't ready to drop the subject yet. "Well, were the English ever on Saint-Luc?"

At that moment, the enormous guide chose to break his silence. "Yes — and no."

"Yes and no?" Dante queried.

"Saint-Luc, this is always French. But, *alors*, in the old times — " He shrugged again. "Yes and no."

"He means everybody was everywhere in the Caribbean, way back," Vanover supplied. "Pirate crews came from all nationalities. Merchants too. There were raids, shipwrecks. You could never be sure where an Englishman or anybody else might end up."

"But in those days a shipwreck was pretty much a death sentence," Adriana pointed out. "None of the sailors even learned how to swim. That was on purpose. They preferred to drown immediately rather than prolong the agony."

"Thank you, Miss Goodnews," put in Kaz, stashing his dive knife in a scabbard on his thigh.

The captain was genuinely impressed. Like the others, he had pegged Adriana as a rich kid who happened to dive because she collected hobbies the same way she collected designer clothes.

"Not a lot of people know that," he said to her. "Been reading up on the Caribbean?"

Adriana flushed. "My uncle is a curator at the British Museum in London. I've spent a couple of summers working for him. You pick stuff up."

Her brow clouded. This year the job had fallen through because Uncle Alfie was in Syria on an archaeological dig. Worse, he had been allowed one assistant, and had chosen Adriana's older brother, Payton. That had left the girl at loose ends, which was a condition never tolerated by the Ballantynes. Adriana's parents spent their summers traveling to hot and trendy places to rub elbows with supermodels, dukes, rock stars, and dot.com tycoons. In all the years she could remember, there had been no summer vacation that she or Payton had spent with the family.

Adriana had a mental picture of her parents shopping their daughter to every museum and research outfit that was prestigious enough to deserve a Ballantyne. Good thing her scuba certification was still current, because Poseidon was about as prestigious as it got. She'd naturally assumed that her family's connections had cinched the job for her, but now she wasn't so sure. None of the others seemed any more qualified than she was, except maybe Star.

As they approached the boundary of the Hidden Shoals, Vanover cut power, and English climbed up to the crow's nest to scan for coral heads that might present a danger to the boat. Here on the reefs, it was not uncommon for towers of coral, reaching toward the sun's nourishing light, to grow until they lurked just below the surface. Over the centuries, many a ship had been fatally holed by such a formation.

At last, they anchored, and preparations for the dive began in earnest. Kaz thought the equipment checks would never end. Tanks charged? Weight belts on? Compressed air coming out of the regulators? Buoyancy compensator vests inflating and deflating properly? It was just like certification class, where they treated you like kindergartners. Did divers ever dive? Or did they spend all their time getting ready?

Dante broke rule number one by trying to walk with his flippers on. He fell flat on his face, nearly smashing his Nikonos underwater camera, which was tethered to his wrist. English helped him up, looking at him pityingly.

Finally, they took to the water, gathering on the surface to pair off.

Kaz spit into his mask to prevent it from fogging. He placed it over his eyes and nose and inhaled to create the watertight suction. He bit down on the regulator and deflated the buoyancy compensator around his neck until he slipped beneath the waves, squeezing the nosepiece of his mask and blowing out to equalize the pressure in his ears.

Underwater. This was only his third dive, and each time he was amazed all over again by this silent alien world, so close at hand, and yet so hidden. People talked about "escaping" into a book or movie. But this was real escape. Down here, hockey was a million miles away, an obscure pastime attached to another life.

His two certification dives had been in cold, murky Lake Simcoe, north of Toronto. So the clear sunlit seascape beneath the surface of the Caribbean was dazzling. The visibility seemed almost infinite, but that wasn't the astonishing part. It was just so *busy* down here, so alive! Steven Allagash's wall-size fish tank was a foggy wasteland by comparison. Thousands of fish of every shape, size, and color darted in all directions.

A tiny, brilliantly striped angelfish ventured up to investigate him. Kaz was fascinated. The curious little creature seemed completely unafraid of the much larger animal that had invaded its ocean. It continued to nose around the bubble stream that rose from his breathing apparatus.

All at once, a shadow passed overhead. In a flash of sudden violence, a round, fat grouper swooped down like a dive-bombing eagle and snapped up the hapless prey.

Whoa. Sorry, guy. Got to keep on your fins. It's a jungle out here.

Almost as an afterthought, he looked around for Dante, his dive partner. To avoid wearing his glasses underwater, the photographer sported a prescription dive mask that distorted his features into a mountainous nose under saucer-wide, staring eyes. It was a shocked, almost crazed appearance. Kaz chuckled — and swallowed water in the process. *Concentrate,* he reminded himself with a cough.

Dante was obviously very impressed by his surroundings, because he was firing off pictures of every shrimp and minnow. Six minutes into the dive, the photographer was officially out of film.

Even through his mask and a cloud of bubbles, English's disgust was plain. Impatiently, he grabbed the two novices each by a wrist and began to swim them toward the reef. Off to the side, they could see the girls moving in the same direction.

As the reef loomed up, the detail of the coral formations began to come into spectacular focus. The colors were unbelievable, almost unreal, like the product of some Hollywood special effects department. The shapes were positively extra-terrestrial: huge plumes of lettuce coral; branched spikes of staghorn; mounds of brain coral the size of dump trucks, all stacked upon each other in a mountain that rose to a summit that was perhaps ten feet below the glittering surface.

Kaz checked the gauge on his diver's watch and realized with some surprise that they had descended to forty feet, which was twice as deep as he'd ever ventured before.

Adriana reached out to touch the coral. In a flash, Star's hand shot forward and grabbed her wrist. The experienced diver gestured with a scolding finger.

I knew that, Kaz thought to himself. The reef was a living organism, composed of uncounted millions of tiny animals called polyps. Even the slightest touch would kill the outermost layer of creatures, damaging the reef. Not to mention that the polyps would sting you.

English flashed the hand signal for descent and led them down to sixty feet, to the base of the coral edifice. Kaz adjusted his B.C. to neutral buoyancy to stop the descent. *I could get good at this,* he reflected, pleased to be developing a talent that had nothing to do with skating, shooting, and attempted murder.

THE DISCOVERY

Here the coral formations gave way to a variety of sea flora growing out of a firm sandy bottom — the Hidden Shoals proper. Life was everywhere, although not quite as colorful as higher up on the reef. At this depth, the sun's rays could not fully penetrate the water. It was a land of twilight.

Kaz's attention was drawn to a small hurried movement below. At first, it seemed as if the sand itself was boiling up into little aquatic dust devils. He angled his body so that his face mask was positioned just above the disturbance and took a closer look.

All at once, the swirling sand was gone, and a large eye was looking back at him.

"Hey!" His cry of shock spit the regulator clear out of his mouth.

It was amazing how loud his voice sounded underwater. And not just to himself, either, because Dante headed straight for him.

A dark slithering blob exploded out of the seabed, leaving a thick cloud of black ink in its wake.

"Octopus!" cried Dante, losing his own regulator in the process.

The identification was unnecessary. Kaz could see the eight undulating arms trailing behind the fleeing body. It was so fluid that the size was hard to guess — maybe a baby pumpkin at the center of a two-foot wingspan.

English flashed out of nowhere, placed himself in the creature's escape path, and allowed it to come to him. He grabbed it by two flailing tentacles. Instantly, the thing turned an angry orange before cloaking itself and the dive guide in a second, much larger emission of ink.

Fumbling for his mouthpiece, Kaz lost sight of them, but caught a glimpse of English, much higher up, carrying his prize to the surface.

Dante pulled a five-by-seven underwater slate out of his B.C. pocket. With the tethered pencil, he scribbled a quick message on the rigid plastic, and showed it to Kaz. It read: DINNER?

Kaz just shrugged.

The dive guide was back almost immediately, but the dark face inside his mask yielded no clue as to the octopus's fate.

At that point, the team had been down for half an hour. English directed them to another section of reef — a gradual upward slope where they could be closer to the surface when their air began to run low. It was important to ascend slowly to avoid decompression sickness. If a diver went up too quickly, the sudden lowering of water pressure was like popping the top on a soda can. Nitrogen gas in the bloodstream could fizz up like a Pepsi. It was no joke — the bends could cripple you for life or kill you.

As he watched the sunlit surface draw closer and closer, Kaz was growing increasingly comfortable. With every passing minute, technique and mechanics became more automatic, allowing him to enjoy the reef and its many inhabitants. *If this keeps up*, he thought, semi-amused, *I could get to like scuba.*

The thought had barely crossed his mind when he saw the silhouette. Alien, yet at the same time familiar, it was approaching from dead ahead — the triangular dorsal fin, the black emotionless eyes, the pointed snout.

Shark.

CHAPTER FOUR

In a split second, his mind sifted through thousands of pictures and diagrams, the nightmare images of a personal library of shark books. A nurse shark, probably. Maybe a reef shark. About four feet long — puny by *Jaws* standards.

But when you come across one, the real thing, with all the fearsome features, all the weapons in the right places —

It never occurred to him to try to swim away or to scramble for the surface. He just hung there, turned to stone, watching the big fish's unhurried approach.

Go away, he pleaded silently. *Don't come near me.*

He could see the teeth now. And he knew, in the absolute core of his being, that this predator was coming for him and him alone.

He would never have believed himself capable of such panic. Before he knew what he was doing, the dive knife was in his hand, and he leaped at the shark, plunging the blade into the soft underside. Strong arms grabbed him from behind, but nothing could stop him now. With a vicious slash, he slit the shark's belly open from stem to stern.

The creature convulsed once, jaws snapping. Then it began to sink, leaving a cloudy trail of blood.

Kaz was spun around, and found himself staring into the furious eyes of Menasce Gérard. The guide gestured emphatically for the surface.

Kaz shook his head. Couldn't he see? The danger was over; the shark was dead.

English did not waste a second command. He placed an iron grip on Kaz's arm, inflated his B.C., and dragged the boy to the surface. They broke to the air thirty yards astern of the *Cortés*.

"Get on the boat!"

Kaz was bewildered. "But it's okay! I got him!"

The guide was in a towering rage. "The boat! *Vite!*"

The five divers moved toward the ship, swimming through the light chop.

As he stroked along, Kaz was still shaking from the excitement of his shark encounter. He felt terrified and pumped up at the same time. He had spent years playing a sport at the very highest level, and yet nothing could have prepared him for the raw exhilaration of a life-and-death struggle. The world had never seemed so vividly alive.

English pulled ahead, his flippers kicking up foam like a paddlewheel. He scrambled onto the dive platform, shed his gear with a single motion, and began hauling his charges out of the water, bellowing like a madman.

Captain Vanover appeared on the deck above them. "What happened?"

English turned blazing eyes on Kaz. "Why do you do this idiot thing? You are maybe crazy? *Fou?*"

Kaz gawked at him. "I was protecting myself!"

"That *petit* guppy wouldn't attack you!"

"How could you know that? He was coming right at me!"

"You move out of the way, *alors!*" English roared. "This is not the rocket science!"

"I'm sorry, okay?" Kaz said defensively. "I'm sorry I interrupted everybody. Let's go back and finish the dive."

"*Oui, bien sûr!*" the guide agreed. "A wonderful idea! After you, monsieur."

Kaz frowned. "What's the problem?" But then he saw it, boiling up from the ocean where they had been diving only minutes before — churning white water around a mass of flailing fins, tails, and sleek bodies. A feeding frenzy — dozens of sharks going after the carcass of the dead one, creating even more carnage with a barrage of snapping jaws.

"Blood in the water, kid," the captain said mildly. "It's like ringing the dinner bell."

All of Kaz's heroic exhilaration morphed into a wave of queasiness. If it hadn't been for English, they would all be in the middle of that, being torn to pieces, thanks to Kaz's mistake.

Now the guide turned on Vanover. "I have not nine lives, me! Why do you send me down with babies? Except the girl." He indicated Star. "She is good. But these three — pah!" And he picked up his equipment, hopped onto the deck, and stormed below.

The four teens remained rooted to the dive platform, unsure of what their next move should be.

The captain couldn't help but notice their intimidation. "Would it make you feel better if I told you he has a heart of gold?"

"He's okay," Star conceded.

"That's because he said you're good," Dante accused.

"I *am* good," she retorted.

The stocky man reached over and began

helping them up to the deck. "I could throttle those pinheads in Hollywood for getting the whole world so hung up on sharks. There's nothing on that reef for a diver to be afraid of. You run into a shark down there, rest assured he's more scared of you than you are of him. Except maybe old Clarence."

Four pairs of ears perked up.

"Clarence?" Kaz echoed, pulling off his dripping flippers.

"Five or six years back," Vanover related, "we had a rush of marlin. You couldn't put a foot in the water without stepping on a fin. The sharks came a few days later. Tiger sharks. Big. They shut this place down for two weeks. Nobody dove, nobody swam, nobody even fished. One pigheaded scientist took a sonar tow out. It came back chicken wire. When the marlin moved on, the sharks followed. No one knows why Clarence didn't go with them. Maybe he was too old to keep up."

"You mean he's still here?" Adriana asked timidly.

"Every few months or so somebody spots him," the captain replied. "He never hurts anyone. Still, you don't fool around with an eighteen-foot tiger shark. But these other reef rats around here — they're harmless."

THE DISCOVERY

The teen divers gazed out over the water to where the feeding frenzy was in full swing.

"Oh, well," Vanover conceded, "if you're going to put blood in the water, all bets are off. Sharks are only human, you know. Your dive knife isn't supposed to be a weapon. It's for cutting your way out of fouled lines and hoses in an emergency. You use it as a last resort. And don't ever pull it on a barracuda. All he'll see is a flash of silver, just like half the fish he eats. He'll take a bite — don't think he won't." Vanover smiled at them benignly. "Now, get out of those wet suits before you roast."

It was a very chastened dive team that sat in a row along the starboard gunwale as the *Hernando Cortés* carried them back to Côte Saint-Luc harbor.

"I knew all that stuff about sharks and barracudas," Star commented. "I just didn't want to be a brownnose."

"Me neither," put in Kaz. "That's why I got the Furious Frenchman mad at me."

"He's scary," Adriana agreed fervently. "Given a choice between him and the sharks, I'll take my chances with the sharks."

"Not me," Dante said feelingly. "Did you catch that story about the tiger shark? They attack humans, don't they?"

Star snorted. "There's a lot of nasty stuff in the ocean. But if you let it spook you, it's like never leaving the house because you never know when a bear is going to wander out of the woods. People dive their whole lives with no problem. So there's a tiger shark somewhere. Big deal. The ocean's full of animals. That's why we take the plunge."

Kaz's eyes fell on an odd piece of equipment mounted on the bulkhead at the base of the Cortés's flying bridge, behind a stack of orange life vests. It looked like a baby's crib that had been taken apart, only the slatted panels were larger, and made of titanium. He had noticed it before, and reflected that the thing was kind of familiar. Now he recognized it — an antishark cage, complete with ballast tanks and control panel.

If sharks are so harmless, why do they need an antishark cage?

Dante interrupted his reverie. "Speaking of animals . . ."

Kaz followed his pointing finger to a large metal bucket sitting just astern of the cockpit. It was filled to the brim with water that kept spilling out with the movement of the boat. They watched, fascinated, as a slate-gray tentacle that matched the galvanized metal of the pail probed tentatively over the rim. A moment later, the octopus hoisted itself up to the edge of the bucket and dropped to the deck. Immediately, it began a quick, amoebalike oozing motion toward the nearest exit. When it spied the four teenagers, it froze for a moment, eyes fixed on them as its body assumed the olive-drab color of the planks.

"Go for it, dude," whispered Dante. "He's going to cook you."

The octopus apparently took that advice to heart. It slithered to the gunwale and promptly disappeared over the side.

As they were unloading equipment on the dock at Côte Saint-Luc harbor, Menasce Gérard had his first look into the empty bucket that had once held his dinner. His frown was a thunderhead.

Adriana read his mind and saw accusation in it. "I swear we didn't do it, Mr. English! He climbed out, ran across the deck, and jumped in the ocean. Honest!"

But once again, the dive guide had retreated into a series of grunts — grunts of suspicion.

17 April 1665

At thirteen years old, Samuel Higgins remembered his mother, but the mental image was fading.

He'd been only six, after all, when Sewell's men had come for him — small enough to be carried off, kicking and howling, in a burlap sack. It was a kidnapping, to be sure, but no constable or sheriff ever came to far-off Liverpool to search for him. What reward might there have been? Samuel's family had nothing. And now six-year-old Samuel had no family.

He would not have been hard to find, if anyone had been looking. Sewell, the chimney sweep, had many climbing boys working for him — all undersized and underfed, abandoned or kidnapped. Samuel, it turned out, excelled at the dirty work. He could scamper up a chimney as easily as walking down the cobblestone alleyways of the port city. And, unlike the boys who worked alongside him, he did not grow long of limb or broad of shoulder as he reached his adolescence.

"Don't worry, lad," laughed old Mr. Sewell over and over, "I've seen a hundred like you. You'll be dead of a fall long before you're too big to climb one of those chimneys."

The man was as sharp as he was heartless, but he turned out to be wrong about that. Samuel never succumbed to the terrible accidents that extinguished the short, unhappy lives of the other boys. And the day did finally come when young Samuel Higgins could no longer fit into the narrow sooty tunnels where he'd earned his keep since he was only six.

"Sorry, lad," Mr. Sewell had told him. "If you do no work, I can't be keeping and feeding you."

It had not been a loving family. But at least he'd belonged. Now he was being driven out. Would the world ever find a place for Samuel Higgins?

Sewell had been hard, but hunger, Samuel's new master, was even harder. At first, he considered a return to the countryside and his mother. But he was not certain where he might find her, or if she was even alive. This life — with Sewell — was the only life he remembered. And now that was over.

His heart yearned for his lost family, but his empty belly was in charge. There was no future in England for a penniless boy except starvation and death. His only hope, his one chance, lay with the sea.

He signed on with the Griffin for a plate of stew and a promise of future wages — not a princely contract, to be sure. But considering that his former employment had come as the result of a kidnapping, this represented freedom, and he was much satisfied. He had no inkling, at that time, of the true purpose of the Griffin and its fleet, nor what its business was in the vast ocean that stretched westward to a new world. He knew only that there was food in the galley for him to eat, and a small rectangle of deck planking outside the captain's quarters where he could sleep. Home.

As the captain's boy, Samuel was the personal manservant to Captain James Blade. His duties included everything from delivering the captain's meals to cleaning and brushing his uniform and wigs, delivering messages to crew members, and emptying the man's chamber pot.

To Captain Blade, Samuel was less than human, a utensil, like a spoon or a shaving razor. "Boy!" he would bark when he needed something. Or often he'd shout, "You!"

The one time that Samuel had the audacity to venture, "My name is Samuel, sir," the captain pulled out a furled snake whip from his belt and smacked him across the side of the head with the bone handle.

"You can ride on this ship or in the waves below — take your choice, boy. But you'll not open your lip to me!"

The blow knocked Samuel clear through the hatch to the captain's quarters, sending a laden tray of food flying every which way.

"And swab this deck!"

There was an emerald the size of a musket ball set in the handle. It left a deep, bloody gash in Samuel's cheek. The wound did not stop oozing until they had passed the Canary Islands.

CHAPTER FIVE

Tad Cutter and his team had been sent from Poseidon's head office in San Diego, California, to map the reefs of the Hidden Shoals northeast of Saint-Luc. Like many scientific undertakings, the results may have been interesting, but harvesting the data was very boring work indeed.

The job consisted of dragging a sonar tow that would measure the depth of the seabed below. To do this over 274 square miles of ocean would take every minute of the eight weeks budgeted for the project. To help them, Cutter and company had been assigned the four teenage interns. But as the early days of summer passed, Kaz, Dante, Adriana, and Star found themselves completely ignored by the Cutter team.

Day after day, the four would awaken in their cabins in the Poseidon compound to find that Captain Bill Hamilton and his *Ponce de León*, the boat assigned to Cutter, were already out there mapping, and had left them behind.

Cutter always had an excuse. "Sorry, guys, but we're just so *busy*. To gather this much data in just a couple of months leaves us no wiggle room. If you're not on board at five A.M., we've got to take off without you."

The next day, they were there at five only to find that the *Ponce de León* had slipped its moorings at four-thirty. The day after that, they arrived at four. There they waited by the boat for three hours before realizing that Cutter and his crew had taken the catamaran to Martinique for supplies.

"We have to complain," argued Dante. "This is our internship, and they're not letting us do it. It's a rip-off."

But there was no one to complain to. Dr. Gallagher was far too busy to see them. And when they ran into him around the institute, he was always lecturing to the video camera that seemed to follow him like a tail. In addition, the director now wore a thick bandage on his forearm, which he carried in a sling. They were all pretty sure it had something to do with his great white shark jaw.

"If he doesn't get away from here fast," Kaz observed, "one of these days that thing is going to come down off the wall and eat him."

Captain Vanover was sympathetic, but not a lot of help. "I know it's lousy, but Tad's probably not doing it on purpose. These research guys — when they get their teeth into a project, they're like zombies. They eat, sleep, and breathe work.

They just can't focus on anything else. Don't let it bum you out. I'm sure your time will come."

"Maybe," grumbled Dante, "but what year?"

Vanover promised to take them out for another dive. But the *Hernando Cortés* was booked almost every day by other scientists, so they would have to wait until the ship was free. In the meantime, the captain agreed to have a word with Bill Hamilton.

The only other person they knew around the institute was English, and no one was in the mood to ask him for favors. Whenever they passed the hulking dive guide in the halls or on the gravel paths of the grounds, they would slink by, and he would look right through them.

"You should talk to him," Dante urged Star. "He likes you."

"He doesn't like anybody," she growled. "He just hates me the least. Besides, he doesn't have any clout around this place."

Poseidon was only a part-time job for English, whose main employment was as a hard-hat diver for the oil rigs off the west side of the island. There his skill and toughness were legendary. He would work at incredible depths of one thousand feet or more, welding underwater pipe and repairing drills and equipment that weighed hundreds of tons.

The more they learned about Menasce Gérard, the more cowed they became.

Their situation did not make for a happy group. Staff members who took pity on them gave them odd jobs to do around the institute. But photocopying, pencil sharpening, and stirring iced tea were not what they had traveled to the Caribbean for.

The others were jealous of Dante, who at least had some meaningful work to do. He got permission to spend a couple of hours in the Poseidon darkroom, developing his underwater photographs. The pictures, though, were a big disappointment. They were excellent wildlife studies, beautifully framed and composed. But the color processing had been so overdone that the pale turquoise Caribbean appeared a deep purple.

"This is the reef?" Star said dubiously, examining the prints. "It looks like outer space."

"It needs to be lighter," Dante agreed.

"It needs to be *blue*," Star amended. "A coral reef is the most beautiful scenery on Earth, not that you can tell from what you shot. You don't have to be a genius to make it look good. Just so long as the water isn't purple."

"I specialize in black and white," Dante admitted sheepishly. "I'm just getting the hang of working with color in the lab."

They were all unhappy, but Adriana was downright miserable. After three summers with her uncle at one of the top museums in the world, this felt a lot like exile.

It was exile, she reminded herself, thinking bitterly of Payton with Uncle Alfie in Syria.

And for what? To run errands for a bunch of oceanography nerds. With the British Museum, she had dug on Roman ruins, translated hieroglyphics, and helped to present a paper at Buckingham Palace. This place was a joke by comparison, and a bad joke at that.

Eventually, though, the gofer jobs would run out, and the four would end up in the tiny village of Côte Saint-Luc, looking to keep busy. It wasn't easy. Since Saint-Luc had no tourism, there was virtually nothing to the town itself. There was a small church with a bell tower, a butcher shop with emaciated chickens hanging upside down in the front, and a dark store with flyspecked windows that sold such strange and random items that Dante had taken to calling it Voodoo "R" Us.

There were two restaurants — a bar and grill that was much more bar than grill, and a European-style café that could have been on any street in Paris.

They preferred the bar and grill because the conch burgers were cheap, and Dante liked to sit

THE DISCOVERY

at the outdoor tables, snapping pictures of the locals with his underwater Nikonos. When there were no passersby, he photographed his three dive mates.

Kaz, who was camera shy, commented, "One more click out of that thing, and it's your nose ring."

"Take me," put in Star. "I've always wanted to be purple."

Dante put down the camera with an exaggerated crash. The boredom and frustration were beginning to set them at one another's throats.

"We've been here a week," said Star, turning her attention to Adriana, "and you have never worn the same pair of shoes twice. How many shoes did you bring? How many shoes do you own?"

"Enough to wedge one where the sun doesn't shine," Adriana snapped back readily.

"Nice shot," chuckled Kaz, his mouth full of fries.

"Mind your own business, rink rat," Star warned. "What do hockey players know, besides how to put each other in the hospital?"

She wasn't sure how, but it was clear that she'd struck a nerve with that comment, because of the deathly quiet of Kaz's reply:

"Don't you ever, ever say that again."

Tempers flared like that regularly. But nothing came to punches; nobody stormed off down Rue de la Chapelle. All four knew that there was nowhere to go.

We're stuck here, Adriana reflected, *out in the back of beyond. We're in this together.*

And suddenly, she was looking straight at it. Across the narrow alley was a tiny neat cottage. The windows were open for ventilation, and in the largest one hung some kind of large wooden sculpture. She couldn't make out exactly what it was, but she had worked at the museum long enough to recognize its age. Time had dulled the sharpness of the carving, the paint was present only in small faded chips, and the wood was weathered and bleached. She had seen pieces like this before — ornate newel posts from mansions and cathedrals that dated back hundreds of years.

She jumped up, almost knocking over her chair. "Guys, you've got to see this!"

They followed her across the dirt lane to the little house.

"It's an eagle," she explained, now that she could see the piece close up.

"What?" asked Star. "That lump hanging in the fishnet? I thought it was a big piece of driftwood."

THE DISCOVERY

"See? Here's the beak and the wings, and the talons are carved in relief against the body," Adriana went on excitedly. "I make it at least three hundred years old, maybe more."

"It's busted," commented Kaz, indicating the jagged break along the eagle's body. "It looks like a giant snapped it off the top of a totem pole."

"Totem poles are North American," Adriana lectured. "I think this came from Europe."

Star looked disgusted. "I know you're, like, wondergirl from some snooty museum, but how could you possibly know something like that?"

"It's oak!" Adriana exclaimed. "There's no oak on Saint-Luc. It's all tropical stuff here. It had to have been brought in by ship. Dante, take a picture. I can scan it at the institute and e-mail it to my uncle."

Dante hefted the camera, grumbling, "You don't need a Ph.D. to tell you what that is. I'll tell you right now." He clicked the shutter. "That's the ugliest thing I've ever seen in my life!"

As Dante spoke, the occupant of the little house appeared in the window. Kaz tried desperately to clamp his hand over the photographer's mouth, but it was too late. The man had heard everything.

It was English.

The enormous guide scowled at them, reached out his long muscular arms, and closed his hurricane shutters with a loud slam.

"Nice timing," snickered Star.

"Oh, why did it have to be *him*?" Dante lamented. "Hey, what are you doing?"

Adriana was marching purposefully to the front door. She rapped smartly and called, "Mr. English, it's us again. Could you please tell us the history of that piece in your window?"

At first, it seemed as if English intended to ignore them. But finally, he thrust open the door, glowering at Adriana.

"You Americans, you have the nerve! You call every shark in the ocean with your macho *stupidité*! Then you steal my octopus! Now you come and insult me in my own home! *Vas-t'en!* This means go away!" And he shut the door in her face.

"I'm from Canada," called Kaz, but he kept his voice low.

Adriana reached out to knock again, but Star grabbed for her wrist. "Forget it. Who cares what he hangs in his window?"

"So long as it isn't us," added Dante feelingly.

But that night, over dinner at the Poseidon commissary, Adriana asked Captain Vanover about the diver's strange window decoration.

THE DISCOVERY

The captain chuckled. "No wonder you couldn't get an answer. I think he's embarrassed about that thing."

"How come?" asked Star.

"It's an old family legend," Vanover explained. "Probably a load of hooey. He'll tell you when he's good and ready." He added, "Or he won't."

"He definitely won't," predicated Dante. "Not after I called it ugly."

Adriana shook her head in amazement. "That piece must be hundreds of years old, and he just hangs it in an open window. I hope he has insurance."

The captain brayed a laugh. "That's a good one — stealing from English!" He noticed Tad Cutter walking to a nearby table. "Hey, Tad — over here."

The blond, blue-eyed man set his tray down at an empty place. "Hey, Braden — guys — "

"Your sonar's been in the water for almost a week now," the captain said amiably. "Why don't you have the kids give it a scrub when they're diving with you tomorrow?"

If Cutter was caught off guard, he didn't show it. "Yeah, it must be pretty crusty with salt by now. Thanks, guys. See you in the morning." He walked off to join his crew.

"He's going to blow us off," Star predicted resentfully. "He says that every night, and he hasn't taken us out once."

"Oh, I know that," the captain agreed. "But if you're going to teach a horse tricks, it helps to be smarter than the horse. Wait till midnight and then go sleep in the boat."

CHAPTER SIX

The R/V *Ponce de León* had four tiny crew cabins belowdecks. Just after midnight, the young divers split up, one to a berth, to wait for dawn and Tad Cutter.

Dante spread his bedroll over the hard bunk and went to sleep — if you could call it that. The waves lapping against the metal hull, while not loud, seemed to echo through the boat with a teeth-jarring quality. Every time he did manage a light doze, his head was pushed against the bulkhead by the motion of the boat in the water.

The *blue* water, Dante reminded himself. *Think in color.*

That was easier said than done. His little "problem" —

That's a private matter! Nobody's business!

The headlines in the clippings in his mother's scrapbook appeared in a collage before his eyes. *13-year-old Wins Adult Photography Prize; Prodigy Behind the Lens; Move Over, Ansel Adams . . .* The critic from the *New York Times* wrote that his use of light and shading was representative of an artist four times his age.

DIVE

And that should have been enough for them, right?

But the next line was always the same: Can you imagine what he'll do with color?

Well, that mystery was over. He knew exactly what he was going to do with color. He was going to butcher it. He was going to make the sea purple.

That's why he had jumped through hoops to learn to dive — a talent he could have been very happy without. A coral reef was the most colorful item on a planet full of color. If the rich hues and tones couldn't reach out to imprint themselves on his artistic sense in this place, then it was never going to happen. And coral reefs didn't exactly turn up on every street corner. You had to go where they were — and that meant underwater.

Quit complaining. You're here. You're diving. You haven't drowned yet . . .

But would they ever get to dive again? Who knew how Cutter would react when he found the four of them lying in wait on the *Ponce de León*?

At long last, sleep claimed him. But it was uneasy sleep, marred by dreams of everything that could go wrong on a dive.

Descend too fast without equalizing pressure . . . bust an eardrum . . . excruciating pain . . .

THE DISCOVERY

He tossed in the narrow berth. Amazingly, that was one of the *milder* diving hazards.

Nitrogen narcosis — the rapture of the deep . . . dissolved nitrogen gas causes a state almost like drunkenness . . .

Dante had never been drunk. But he was pretty sure a hundred feet below the waves wasn't the place to do it. There were horror stories of "narced" divers who actually forgot which way was up until they ran out of air and drowned. But that still wasn't the ultimate scuba nightmare.

The bends . . . bubbles in the bloodstream . . . tiny time bombs in the body . . . all you can do is wait to see if you're crippled for life or even . . .

"Killed!" He sat bolt upright in his bunk. The *Ponce de León* was moving. He could feel and hear the thrum of the engine.

He opened dry crusty eyes and found himself gawking at the most beautiful woman he'd ever seen — tall and tan, with long dark — brown? — hair.

She seemed just as surprised to see him. Then she smiled. "Look, Chris," she called through the low hatch. "Stowaways."

A bearded man appeared beside her, his arms laden with gear. He looked at Dante in dismay. "The kids!"

"We're all here," Dante managed, trying to keep from staring at her. "Tad said you wanted our — help."

She grinned even wider — a magazine cover smile. "I'm Marina Kappas, Poseidon, San Diego. The sourpuss here is Chris Reardon." She held out her hand. "We could really use you today."

Dante scrambled from his bedroll and shook it. It was electric just touching her. "Dante. Dante Lewis."

"The photographer!" she beamed. "I'm really excited to take a look at some of your work."

Reardon seemed bewildered by the friendly exchange. "Marina — can I talk to you?"

"Not now."

"But — "

A cloud passed briefly over her perfect features. "I said not now. Why don't you go on deck and tell Tad the good news."

Dante set about rousing his teammates with the information that they had been discovered.

"You mean Cutter walked right in on you?" asked Kaz, scrambling out of his bunk.

"Not Cutter — Marina." Dante couldn't resist adding, "Wait till you see her!"

"Was she mad?" Adriana probed.

"Actually, she seemed kind of happy to see

me," he replied honestly. "Her friend wasn't all that thrilled, though."

Topside, they introduced themselves to Bill Hamilton, captain of the *Ponce de León*. Cutter was half buried in the motor of a Brownie floating air compressor, tinkering with a wrench.

Noticing them, the team leader grunted, "Good. You're up. You'll be logging a lot of dive time today — too much for scuba. But this big baby can keep you down there for hours."

Their uneasiness quickly turned to confusion. Cutter was acting as if their presence today was not only expected, but vital. As if he *hadn't* been dodging them for close to a week!

Kaz spoke up. "It takes so long to clean a sonar tow?"

"Oh, I checked that; it's fine," Cutter assured them. "We need you for something much more important. There are a lot of caves down there that the sonar won't pick up. We need you to find them for us."

"And explore them?" Star asked eagerly.

Cutter shook his head. "Too dangerous. Just tag the mouth with one of these marker buoys. That'll fire off a float to the surface. Then we'll catalog the location from topside. Got it?"

There was genuine excitement as the four divers suited up.

"Maybe we were wrong about Cutter and his people," Adriana suggested, pulling the thin wetsuit material until it fit snugly at her wrists. "It looks like they're really going to let us do some work this summer."

Star was skeptical. "I've seen a lot of reef maps. They don't have caves marked on them."

"This one will," put in Dante, detaching his regulator from its tank. On this dive, they would be breathing air directly from the Brownie, via long flexible hoses. "Remember, Poseidon's number one. They do everything to the max."

Seeing Star limp as she stepped into the lightweight suit, Marina rushed over to steady her.

Star wheeled away. "What do you think you're doing?"

Her outrage was so genuine, so harsh, that the researcher was struck momentarily dumb.

"Leave her alone, Star — " Dante began.

"Do you think I'm a beginner at this?" Star persisted.

Marina found her voice at last. "I saw you stumble. It happens to everyone in rolling seas — even top divers."

"Thou shalt not help Star," Kaz intoned apologetically. "That's kind of the eleventh commandment around here."

The slight girl glared at him as Marina went

back to help Cutter with the compressor. "You're *hot* for her! You too, Dante!"

"So what if we are?" Dante shot back at her. "You're our dive partner, not our mother. What's it to you?"

Star's anger did not fade until she had slipped beneath the choppy surface. It was impossible to stay mad down here, in the crystalline waters, passing through a school of chromis, swimming in tight formation, an orange cloud.

Sure, she was sensitive about her handicap. But she certainly couldn't blame Marina Kappas for being beautiful — or Dante and Kaz for noticing.

Anyway, underwater, Star Ling had no handicap. This was her medium, the world her body had been designed for. She slowly fan-kicked her flippers on the descent. If, at that moment, she had suddenly woken up with amnesia, she would have noticed no weakness at all on her left side. And that was exactly the way she liked it.

The reef here was fairly shallow — only about forty feet at its deepest — and flatter than the dive site they had visited with Vanover and English. But life and color were everywhere. Decorating the coral were fire-engine-red sponges, towering sea fans, and starfish the size of throw rugs. Snakelike trumpet fish, multihued creatures straight out of Dr. Seuss, stabbed down from above, feeding on the polyps. A curious tetra darted around the safety line hooked to her belt. She chased it away with a flurry of bubbles.

"Hey!"

The sound carried so well through the water that she recognized Dante's voice. She spied the young photographer not far away, hovering neutrally buoyant, waving wildly. As she swam closer, she spied the cause of his excitement — a black hole in the limestone seafloor about the circumference of a prizewinning watermelon.

He calls that a cave?

Pulling her slate out of the B.C. vest, she scribbled *TOO SMALL*. But Dante shook his head and began fumbling with one of the marker buoys on his belt. He lost his grip on the cartridge, and it floated to the sand at the mouth of the opening.

Dante reached down to recover it.

Now it was Star's turn to shout aloud. "No!"

THE DISCOVERY

CHAPTER SEVEN

Just as Dante's glove closed over the cartridge, the grotesque head of a moray eel exploded out of the hole, revealing an improbably gaping mouth of inch-long needles. Shocked, he snapped back his arm, and the jaws bit down on the metal of the marker buoy, sending broken teeth in all directions.

In a panic, Dante dropped the cartridge and reached for the valve of his B.C. Star grabbed him before he could inflate the vest and shoot upward.

She pushed her mask right up against his, communicating her message with dark eyes: *Calm down. It didn't happen. You're okay.*

Dante nodded, gasping into his regulator. He was a pretty crummy diver, Star reflected, but sometimes luck was more important than skill. The big eel could have taken a substantial chunk of flesh out of his hand.

Not far away, Kaz and Adriana were tagging a cave entrance with another one of the marker buoys. There was a pop followed by a hiss, and the float rocketed to the surface.

One down and five hundred to go, Star thought to herself. She still couldn't figure out why Tad Cutter needed this. To map every grotto and nook in a reef system the size of Hidden Shoals would take years, not a couple of months. It didn't make sense.

She was enjoying the chance to dive without the bulky scuba tank. It was a feeling of freedom, although she was tethered to the Brownie by her air hose and safety line. Soaring and swooping with the fish, pretending to be one of them — it was a childish game, but Star never got tired of it.

She swam with a school of mackerel until they were scattered by a big loggerhead turtle. The loggerhead's stony shell felt ancient against her gloved hand — a piece of prehistory here in the twenty-first century.

She spotted Kaz hovering over another cave, unclipping a fresh marker buoy from his belt. He wasn't much of a diver either, she reflected. But there was an ease, almost a grace to his movements — something only natural athletes had.

As Star watched him work, a large barracuda loomed up behind the boy.

Should I signal him?

She remembered the incident with the shark. Kaz was easily spooked, and might do something stupid. Besides, barracudas never attack humans on purpose.

But the seven-footer was nosy. Star bit her tongue as the protruding lower jaw probed right up behind Kaz, the gleaming teeth mere inches from the back of his neck.

All at once, Kaz turned around, coming face to jaws with the notorious predator. Shocked, he triggered the marker buoy. The pop startled the barracuda, and it turned tail and darted away. Star laughed, sending clouds of bubbles rushing for the surface.

Adriana was nearby, paralleling the bottom, trying to shoo away an aggressive triggerfish. She was a little more comfortable in the water than Kaz — a tourist rather than a beginner. The girl had obviously done some diving on high-priced vacations in the past.

It bugged her. Not that Adriana was rich, but that Poseidon had matched Star with such unqualified teammates.

Then again, how could they be sure I was any good? They knew about my cerebral palsy. . . .

It was almost as if Poseidon had gone after weak divers on purpose.

"Look!" came a cry.

Dante again. If the boy didn't stop yelling underwater, he was going to drink enough salt to give himself high blood pressure.

He was pointing and waving — probably at another rabbit hole he considered a cave. But when she swam to his side, he was gazing into the distance, where the reef fell off into deeper water.

She squinted, trying to zoom in on the object of his interest. Light, and therefore visibility, diminished with depth. She shot him an expansive shrug. Because of the need to communicate without words, divers often used exaggerated gestures like stage actors playing to the back row.

Dante deflated his B.C., descending into the twilight. Star followed. A tug at her belt told her that the safety line had become taut, and that they were now pulling the Brownie along with them. She glanced over her shoulder and saw that the others had noticed it too. Kaz and Adriana finned after them.

What does Dante think he sees? There was such a thing as an underwater mirage. His magnified eyes behind his mask gave him a deranged appearance. It was easy to believe he was hallucinating.

And then she spotted it.

In the middle of this most natural of settings, it was jarring to see something so artificial, so man-made. The sunken airplane sat in the sand, its fuselage partially encrusted with coral and sea life. One wing had broken off on impact with the water. It lay a short distance away, hidden by seaweed.

Star's heart began to pound so hard she was afraid it might burst her wet suit. This was the ultimate diver's prize. A wreck! She had read about this experience in scuba magazines. But the excitement of the real thing went far beyond anything she could have imagined.

She approached slowly, reverently, half expecting the plane to vanish just as she reached out to touch it. Never had she imagined this could happen to her — and certainly not when she was teamed up with a bunch of landlubbers like this bunch! The others hung back, watching her uncertainly.

When she spotted the insignia on the side, a gasp escaped her — a larger bubble among the many smaller ones. The marking was obscured by anemone growth, but it was unmistakable. A swastika. This was a German warplane from World War II!

She swam over to peer into the cockpit, wondering if she'd see a skeleton at the controls. But, no. The big bomber was deserted.

The windshield was shattered, providing a narrow entryway to the downed plane.

Star hesitated. Wreck diving could be dangerous.

But this is the chance of a lifetime!

She entered the cockpit and squeezed between the pilot's and copilot's chairs into the body of the plane. The space was tiny — it was hard to believe that an entire crew of grown men had flown in this cigar box. Just a few feet into the fuselage and she was in near-total darkness. The only light was from two turrets of bulletproof glass. Out of each pointed a swiveling machine gun, harmless now, encased in a layer of coral. It was a grim reminder that this silent metal husk was once an instrument of war, a delivery system for death.

She snaked back toward the bomber's tail. Here, there was absolute blackness, and the walls closed in until she was in the narrowest of tunnels.

As she reversed course, her flipper caught on the low ceiling and came off. Alert, she was able to trap it between her legs. Putting it on again in the cramped space was a major operation, and she was surprised at how exhausted it left her. Her bubbles, trapped below the ceiling of the craft, converged to form a small pocket of air.

I'd better get out of here.

But not without a souvenir — some kind of

proof that she'd been there. *Artifacts*, the wreck divers called them. Plates and silverware from sunken ships were especially prized. But what to take from a plane? She couldn't exactly snap off a three-hundred-pound propeller.

Once again, her eyes fell on the machine gun. A full strap of ammunition dangled from the carbine, waving lightly in the current.

She crawled rather than swam up to it, grasping holds on the floor of the cabin. Popping the shells out was easier than she expected — the old strapping fell apart on contact, and the bullets dropped into her glove. The thrill of their touch was almost tangible.

World War II in the palm of your hand, she reflected. *Hey —*

Fiddling with the gun had disturbed the layer of silt that covered the plane. A storm of swirling brown particles filled the turret. The bullets slipped through her fingers and disappeared.

Going after her prize was instinct. Any diver would have done the same thing. She ducked into the cloud as if bobbing for apples. That was when she felt it — no flow of compressed gas from the demand regulator between her teeth.

She was out of air.

CHAPTER EIGHT

No! Star thought desperately. *Impossible! I'm not breathing out of a tank!*

The truth came to her in an icy shot of fear. A kink in her hose! Her air supply must have caught on something — a knob, a handle. But where? A frantic glance toward the back of the cabin revealed only darkness.

She tugged gently but insistently at the hose, hoping to jar it free. The life-giving gas would not come. *Come on!* She yanked harder, knowing all the while it was a bad idea, that she was likely to foul the supply even further.

Star Ling was such a confident diver that when panic came, the feeling was completely alien to her. Her first inclination was to spit out her mouthpiece and shoot for the surface, but when she tried to crawl out the opening in the gun turret, her tether line held her back. She was trapped in this submerged metal coffin.

She pulled out her knife and began to flail blindly behind her, but she couldn't see anything in the billowing storm of silt.

It was the glint of the steel blade in the gun

turret that told Kaz something was wrong. When Star saw him swimming toward her, she realized he was her only hope. She gestured madly with her finger across her throat — the diver's signal for *no air*.

It seemed to take forever for him to get there. *Water acts as a magnifying glass,* she reminded herself. *He looks closer than he is.*

The thought was little comfort. She was close to unconsciousness, her field of vision darkening at the edges. She struggled to stay alert. Would this hockey player even know what to do when he reached her?

He's paddling with his hands, for God's sake! A mistake right out of Diving 101!

And then he was right there. She caught a glimpse of herself reflected in his mask and realized just how far gone she was. Her face was ashen, her eyes bulging in horror. She could not hold on much longer. The blackness was overtaking her.

Kaz sucked hard on his regulator, then spat it out and forced the mouthpiece between Star's blue lips. The delicious blast of air snapped her back from the edge of the void. She breathed deeply, fighting to keep herself from hyperventilating.

Kaz crawled in through the opening in the turret and searched the floor of the plane. He fanned the water to disperse the curtain of silt. When he spied her regulator, he grasped the problem immediately. The hose had wrapped itself around the bombardier's joystick so tightly that the flow of air had been cut off. The snarl was complicated further by Star's safety line, which was tangled up with the air supply and also snagged on a hook above the bailout hatch. Kaz used his knife to cut the line, then freed the hose and breathed from the mouthpiece.

Star watched him in wonder. The boy was an awkward diver, but in this crisis, his actions were swift and decisive. *Must be the hockey training,* she thought grudgingly. She hated to admit it, but Bobby Kaczinski had very probably just saved her life.

She could feel herself trembling in spite of the warm water. The incident had rattled her — but not enough to keep her from grabbing another handful of bullets as they exited the plane.

They surfaced beside the Brownie and held on, rolling with the choppy seas.

Dante was already shouting as he spat out his mouthpiece. "Are you okay?"

"Don't tell anybody what happened!" Star ordered. "Not Cutter — nobody!"

"What *did* happen?" asked Adriana. "It looked like you got stuck in that plane."

"If they don't trust our diving, they'll ground us in a heartbeat!" Star persisted. "*Promise!*"

Kaz was thunderstruck. "Is that all you've got to say? You could be dead right now!"

"I got in a jam and my partner helped me out of it," Star insisted. "That's how the buddy system's supposed to work."

"This is only my fourth dive!" Kaz sputtered. "My second in the ocean! What if I messed up? They don't teach that in scuba class, Star! What if I didn't know what to do? I'd have to live with that!" The image of Drew Christiansen, lying prostrate on the ice, came to him, and he fell silent. How much guilt could fit on one conscience?

"Don't you realize what we just saw?" cried Star. "People dive their whole lives and never find a wreck!" She turned to Dante. "That's some set of eagle eyes you've got! Maybe we're all crazy and water really *is* purple."

"I just" — he paused, uncomfortable — "got lucky."

"A German plane!" exclaimed Adriana. "Maybe it's from one of the famous bombing runs on Curaçao. It's a real find for the historical community."

"It's a real find for *us*," Star corrected sharply. She unzipped the pouch on her dive belt and came up with the handful of bullets. "And we've got the artifacts to prove it. I can't wait to rub these in Cutter's face. Let's see if he treats us like a bunch of tadpoles now!"

Since the *Ponce de León* was combing the reef with its sonar tow, the four had to wait on the floating Brownie for the research vessel to pass by. Dante spotted it almost immediately, a tiny blip in the heat shimmer on the horizon. Twenty minutes later, the ship was pulling alongside them.

Kaz saw Chris Reardon first, half asleep in the stern, a fishing rod in his hand, trawling for tuna over the gunwale. "Hey, Chris!" he called.

Reardon let out a loud belch, but otherwise gave no indication he'd heard.

"Get that rod out of the water!" a sharp voice ordered him. "You'll skewer one of the kids!"

Marina was rushing down to the dive platform to help them aboard. She frowned at the two marker buoys bobbing in the waves. "I know there are a lot more caves than that."

"Dante found a wreck!" Star panted.

The researcher's eyes were instantly alert. "A wreck?"

"A World War II airplane," Adriana supplied.

"Look!" Star thrust a fistful of coral-encrusted bullets in Marina's face.

Marina stared for a moment, and then her supermodel's features relaxed into an amused grin. "Star, that's not — "

But Star was already limping toward the main companionway, calling, "Tad!" The others followed her, wet suits dripping.

Tad Cutter was seated at the foldaway table in the galley, poring over an endless data printout on continuous form paper.

"There's a plane down there," Star told him excitedly. "A German bomber." She slammed the machine gun bullets onto the computer.

Cutter looked from the bullets to their earnest faces and laughed — full-throated guffaws that filled the salon.

"Hey!" Star was insulted. "You may think we're a bunch of pests to be ignored, but we know what a plane looks like!"

"No!" the team leader managed, struggling to regain his control. "You guys are right. There's a plane down there. But it's not from World War II."

"Yes, it is," Adriana insisted. "A Messerschmidt bomber, propeller driven, with a swastika and German cross markings. The Nazis used them in the Caribbean against Allied oil-drilling operations."

"And that's exactly what the movie was about — a German bomber that crashed into the sea," Cutter informed them. "The studio folks built an exact model of a Messerschmidt, towed it out here, and sank it on the reef. *That's* what you found. Not a wreck — a Hollywood set."

Star's face fell the distance between an undiscovered wreck and an underwater phony. The others looked on in dismay. A minute ago it seemed as if they had earned the respect of Cutter and his crew. Now they were nobodies again.

The blond man picked up one of the bullets. "This isn't nearly enough coral growth for an artifact from World War II. After sixty years, the whole shell casing would be covered, most likely. This looks about right for three years on the reef — the time since that movie got made."

Marina appeared at the companionway. "Don't take it so hard. You're not the first divers to find that plane and think it was something special. I doubt you'll be the last." She smiled. "There are a lot of caves down there. We'll need you back in the water as soon as possible. Use the oxygen to help you outgas. It's topside — the tanks with the green labels."

Since the body absorbs some of the nitrogen from compressed air at depth, it was important to expel that nitrogen before diving again the same day. Breathing pure oxygen sped up the whole process.

On deck, Dante pulled a tank from the rack, struggling under its weight.

Kaz frowned at the other boy. "She said green labels."

"Yeah?"

"These are red."

"Oh — right." Embarrassed, Dante fumbled with the cylinder and dropped it. Kaz got his foot out of the way a split second before the heavy metal hit the deck.

Dante grimaced. "Sorry." That was becoming a pretty useful word for him. *Sorry for nearly shattering your toe; sorry for handing you a tank of God-knows-what that might have poisoned you; sorry for spotting the plane that almost became Star's tomb.* There was no question about it. He stank at this internship. And not just the diving part. Everything he did around here turned out to be wrong.

Kaz hauled out four of the oxygen cylinders and the divers divided them up. He placed the clear plastic mask over his mouth and nose and turned on the valve. "It isn't so bad, right?" he asked, his voice muffled. "I mean, we look like idiots, but they still want us to tag caves for them. At least we didn't lose our jobs."

"I still say something's fishy about that," put in Star. "We've got two markers in the water. Have any of those guys even bothered to record their positions?"

In answer, a loud snore came from the stern of the boat, as Reardon continued his hunt for a prizewinning tuna.

Adriana placed the mask over her face and then withdrew it, licking her dry lips thoughtfully. "The only thing that bothers me is that they're supposed to be doing a sonar scan, right? Mapping the reef. But the data Cutter's studying isn't sonar data."

Kaz snapped to attention. "It isn't?"

"One summer, the British Museum had a team searching for ancient Roman artifacts in the Thames River — shields, helmets, armor. They used a side-scan magnetometer to pick up signs of metal underwater. Well, the data from that scan is exactly like the data on Cutter's table."

Star snapped her fingers. "They're looking for something in the ocean. Something metal."

Dante was confused. "Then why do they want us down there marking caves?"

All at once, a wide smile of understanding appeared on the slight girl's face. "It's bell work!"

"Bell work?" repeated Adriana.

"When I was in fifth grade," Star explained,

"my teacher always put a few math problems on the board for when we came in after the bell. It wasn't stuff we had to know — not on any test or anything. It was just supposed to keep us busy while she finished her coffee in the faculty room. That's what this cave thing is all about — they're keeping us busy while they're searching!"

The four divers exchanged solemn glances. Could it really be true? They knew Cutter and his team had little respect for them, but could the researchers be manipulating them this way?

Kaz broke the uneasy silence. "Okay, let's say both you guys are right. They're jerking us around, keeping us busy doing nothing, while they're scanning the Hidden Shoals for metal. That still doesn't answer the biggest question — why all this secrecy? These people are scientists working for a top institute. Why can't they just admit what they're after?"

Adriana flipped her wet hair out of her face. "It seems to me," she said slowly, "that there must be something very special about their work."

Dante raised an eyebrow. "A government contract? Maybe top secret?"

"Maybe," she said. "But whatever it is, we're mixed up in it now."

03 July 1665

At first, Samuel blamed the stink of the Griffin on the port of Liverpool. But as they sailed farther, in fair seas or rough, the overpowering stench was still with them. Worse, it seemed to be growing in intensity. It was a mixture of bilge water, cooking fires, the rotting food stores, and livestock smells from the goats, pigs, and chickens that were raised on board to keep up a supply of fresh milk, eggs, and meat for the captain and crew.

Mostly, though, it was the reek of people — two and eighty unwashed men on a long journey under a relentless sun. The acrid odor of seasickness could never be fully swabbed away. And as the barque was tossed by malevolent waves, even the most seasoned sailor would lose control of his stomach. Captain Blade himself was not immune. One time during a spell of rough weather, Samuel barged in on him on the floor of his quarters, retching into his chamber pot.

He leaped to his feet, scorching Samuel with eyes of fire. "You'll not speak of this to anyone, boy, or I'll have you flogged!"

It was not an idle threat. There were floggings almost daily on the crew deck of the Griffin. Captain Blade insisted on performing these himself, with his bone-handled snake whip.

"Ah, it feels good to stretch the old muscles," he would grin as his victim sobbed in a pool of his own blood, his back crisscrossed with angry red stripes. "A man needs some physical activity."

A regular recipient of Blade's brand of "physical activity" was old Evans, the sail maker. The overpowering wind gusts of the Atlantic crossing relentlessly shredded the barque's many sails. Though the silver-haired man labored night and day, sewing until he could barely see his stiff fingers before his failing eyes, he could not keep up with the damage.

"I'll hang your courtly self if I don't see the mizzen in its place before the boy brings my supper!" the captain roared. "Courtly" was the ultimate insult on shipboard. A courtly seaman was a landlubber.

In Evans's case it was the truth. He was a farmer by trade. His landlord had evicted him from the potato fields that provided his meager living. Evans had grown too weak to work the property profitably, and he had no sons to help him. Going to sea was his only chance to provide for his wife and daughters.

In spite of their age difference, Samuel felt a bond with the much older man. Both were non-sailors who had been forced by poverty to the Griffin and its merciless captain. The ship's boy spent most of his free time in the sail maker's cabin, stitching canvas until his hands bled, substituting his young eyes for the old man's dim ones.

Although Evans appreciated the help, he must have at first suspected that Samuel was the captain's spy. The old man was always saying things like, "Captain James Blade is a right gentleman. Lucky we are to have such a fine master on the Griffin."

Even after a brutal flogging, he had nothing but praise for the instrument of his agony. As Samuel poured seawater over the man's whip-scarred back to prevent infection, Evans would whimper, "'Tis a fine captain who takes such a personal interest in the affairs of his crew."

Samuel said nothing. He had never known his own father, and longed for the moment that Evans would trust him with his true thoughts.

Late one night, as the two struggled to darn a foresail so pockmarked by mending that it resembled a ragamuffin's wardrobe, the moment finally came. By the dim flicker of a waterlogged oil lamp, Evans said in a matter-of-fact tone, "He's a proper lunatic, that captain of ours. I hate him, I do."

"Shhh!" Samuel hissed, glancing nervously over his shoulder. Then, in a whisper, "I hate him too. Every time I touch his filthy chamber pot, I want to throw it in his face."

"That whip — I see it in my sleep!" All at once,

the old man's moist, haunted eyes took on a faraway look. "In my dream, it's wrapped around Blade's white throat. I'm pulling it tighter, tighter. He screams, but I don't stop pulling, squeezing — "

"That's mutiny!" Samuel breathed in horror. "It's a hanging offense!"

"And then I think of my girls," the old man finished, visibly deflated, "and I remember I have to avoid the noose for their sakes." He added earnestly, "But this old body is not strong enough to survive another flogging. I'm telling you true, Samuel. I'll die under James Blade's lash."

The weather continued wild and dangerous. Two and a half months into the perilous crossing, a storm sank the *Viscount,* an eighteen-gun brigantine in their small fleet. The *Griffin* picked up four and thirty hapless sailors, adrift in the rough seas. The rest simply slipped beneath the waves and were seen no more. Captain Blade clung to the ratlines through the entire operation, cracking his whip into the wind and rain and hurling abuse at rescuers and survivors alike.

There were now more than one hundred souls packed onto the barque. Conditions were more than cramped; they were unsafe. Fever spread like wildfire through the seething mass of humanity. Six men had already died, including the ship's carpenter, whose responsibilities included replacing damaged or rotten *wood in the leaky hull. The* Griffin *sat low in the water. Samuel was ordered away from the sail maker's cabin to join the army of pumpers in the unbreathable air of the reeking bilge.*

He was returning, bowed down with fatigue, from several hours below, when he heard the distant cry: "Sail, ho!"

It was Evans, perched high in the rigging, where he had been struggling to mend a tear in the square topsail at the tip of the mainmast. From that vantage point, he had spied another ship on the horizon.

Captain Blade poked his head out of his quarters. "One of ours?" he called.

Evans squinted. "I can't tell, sir!"

Blade stormed down to the main deck. "Are you a seaman or a gooseberry, mister? Is it one of our fleet?"

Samuel tried to jump to the old man's defense. "He doesn't know ships, sir! He's just a farmer who went to —"

Thwack! The big emerald flashed in the sun as the captain brought the bone handle of his whip down hard on Samuel's forehead. He collapsed to his knees, seeing stars.

"You'll earn yourself a flogging if I have to come up there!" Blade bellowed at his sail maker.

But Evans was paralyzed. His pale, nearsighted eyes could not recognize the distant vessel, and his fear of the captain prevented him from guessing.

THE DISCOVERY

"You'll be right sorry you troubled me!" Blade *strode to the ratlines and began to climb, not quickly, but with the authority and balance that comes from decades spent on shipboard.*

It was a nightmare, Samuel reflected, watching the captain close in on the quaking sail maker. His friend's words came back to him: "This old body isn't strong enough to survive another flogging. . . ."

He flung himself at the ratlines, scrambling like a spider, shocked at first at how fast and good he was at it. The chimneys, *he thought, arms and legs working efficiently.* If I can make it up Sewell's chimneys, I can make it up anything!

The captain bellowed with rage as he pulled level with Evans. "Why, you worthless maggot, don't you recognize your own flagship? I'll flog you till there's nothing left but a handful of your rotting teeth!"

The angry green of the emerald flashed in the sun. At first, Samuel thought Blade was going to lash the poor farmer right there on the ratlines. It was a horrifying prospect. Surely Evans would lose his grip and fall. Then he realized that it was the old sail maker who had snatched up the whip, and was attempting to wrap it around Blade's neck.

"No!" Samuel cried, but he knew it was already too late. Under maritime law, even touching the captain was a capital crime. No matter what happened now, poor Evans would hang.

"*Mutinous — scum —* " With great strength, *Blade managed to pull himself free. He brought down his clasped hands full force on the sail maker's crown. Evans went rigid for a moment, and then let go of the rope. Horrified, Samuel watched his only friend plunge to his death one hundred feet to the deck below.*

The effort of the savage blow had overbalanced the captain, and, with a terrified scream, he too lost his purchase on the ratlines.

I'll not help him, *Samuel resolved as his master plummeted toward him.* I'll not save the murdering —

Yet the action was pure instinct. As the captain fell, pawing desperately at the rigging, Samuel reached out and grabbed his belt. He would not have been able to hold on, but he slowed the acceleration of the drop just enough for Blade to snatch the webbing of rope. The cruel captain hung on, gasping for breath and whimpering with panic, as crewmen surrounded the sail maker's broken body beneath them.

It should be you, Captain, lying down there dead, and Evans up here with me, consigning your black soul to the devil! *Samuel thought, biting back tears. Aloud, he just said,* "You all right, sir?"

Gingerly, Blade hoisted himself up to regard his cabin boy. "You're my lucky angel, boy," *he groaned wearily.* "Aye, you're a lucky one, Samuel Higgins."

THE DISCOVERY

CHAPTER NINE

Slowly but surely, Kaz, Adriana, Dante, and Star began to fit into the routine at Poseidon Oceanographic Institute. They continued to dive with Cutter and his crew aboard the *Ponce de León*, tagging underwater caves and trying to keep a low profile while they snooped.

"We don't want them to think we're on to them," Star advised. "No matter what they're up to."

Dante was all for the interns minding their own business. "If it's top secret or something," was his reasoning, "then it should stay that way."

"We're just curious," Kaz insisted. "It's not like we're spies."

"And who has a better right to know?" Star added. "They're messing up our summer program. The least they can do is tell us why."

So they continued with their busywork and kept an eye on the team from San Diego, although there was little to see. According to Captain Vanover, a magnetometer looked pretty much like a sonar, so the tow fish itself yielded no clue. Cutter spent most of his time belowdecks, his

DIVE

head buried in reams of printouts. Reardon could have been any fishing bum on a Caribbean vacation. He seldom left the stern and his rod and reel. Captain Hamilton ran the boat, period. Marina was the only one who had much interaction with the teen divers.

"If anybody's innocent on Cutter's team, it has to be her," was Adriana's opinion. "She's just a friendly, interested mentor."

"Who looks like a supermodel," finished Kaz.

"You don't have to be a photographer to recognize *that* thing of beauty," Dante agreed.

Star shook her head. "You guys are such losers."

It was not the first piece of ribbing Dante had taken on the subject. When he printed his second batch of pictures, more than half of them were of Marina. To make matters worse, the developing was so off that her perfect skin matched the bright orange of the fire coral in the reef shots.

"Stick to purple water, Romeo," was Adriana's opinion.

The interns kept their suspicions to themselves, saying nothing to the other institute people for fear of word getting back to Cutter. When they did ask questions, they kept them general, omitting any reference to the team from California.

"Why would a ship tow a side-scan magnetometer?" Adriana asked Captain Vanover in the cafeteria one night.

"Depends who's on board, and what he's looking for," came the reply. "A mag is basically a fancy metal detector. Geologists say most of the world's mineral ore is under the sea."

"Mining companies use them?" asked Kaz.

"Sometimes. But the salvage people love them too — anybody who wants to track down something big underwater. How do you think they found the *Titanic*? The military is also a big user. They're always going after stuff — equipment and ordnance they lost in the drink."

Dante shot the others a meaningful glance. Could that be the mysterious assignment — top secret work for the navy, searching for a sunken submarine or even a lost nuke?

"But around here," Vanover went on, "a lot of the mag scans are done by treasure hunters."

"Treasure hunters?" repeated Star.

"Sure," the captain told them. "A few hundred years ago, these waters were the money highway. And they say at least half of it is lying under the seabed somewhere."

Adriana nodded wisely. "In the sixteenth and seventeenth centuries, the Spanish shipped billions in treasure from the New World back to Spain."

"A lot of those ships never made it to Europe," Vanover explained. "Hurricanes, reefs, pirates. That's why a mag comes in handy. Gold and silver are *metals*. If a galleon went down in the area, its cargo would show up on the scan."

Dante was amazed. "And that works? You just tow it around till you get a hit, and bring up millions?"

The captain laughed. "It's a little more complicated than that, Dante. First of all, the sea is a big place — three quarters of the earth's surface, remember? Second, most of those wrecks are under thousands of feet of ocean, far too deep for any diver to reach them. But even if a wreck is located in shallow water, it's not like there would be a boat full of gold bars just sitting there in the sand. Those old ships were made of wood. Most of that would be gone by now, eaten little by little by microscopic worms in the water. And pretty much all that's left is buried in coral, which is another problem. It's against the law to destroy a living reef."

"In other words, forget about it," concluded Kaz.

"Most treasure hunters search for decades and never find much," Vanover agreed. "But there are exceptions. A man named Mel Fisher excavated two galleons off the Florida Keys, and brought up hundreds of millions in gold and gems."

Dante whistled. "He's got it made!"

"Not necessarily," said the captain. "Who owns sunken treasure? Now the government's suing him, and he's up to his ears in lawyers."

"A hundred million bucks can hire a lot of lawyers," Dante pointed out. "That's not just rich; it's *rolling*."

Huge money — that was Dante's secret dream. Not that most people didn't want to get rich. But for an artist, a big pile of cash had a special meaning — freedom. He could pursue his craft without having to worry about selling pictures or making a living.

A financially secure photographer wouldn't have to learn color. Which had one definite advantage in Dante's eyes.

No diving.

Dante was the weakest diver in the group, but even his meager skills were improving. This was true for all of them, if for no other reason than the huge amount of ocean time they were logging.

"You learn to dive by diving," was Star's opinion. "Even a baboon would get better if he spent as much time underwater as us."

When it came to scuba, Star held on to her

praise the way a miser holds on to his pennies. To listen to her, the only people who had ever gotten it right were herself, English, and Jacques Cousteau, probably in that order.

It bugged Kaz. *She thinks we're all useless,* he reflected resentfully. *I probably saved her life in that plane, and she never even said thanks.*

In fact, Star was very much aware of Kaz's development as a diver. His technique was raw, but the Canadian's natural athletic ability gave him amazing strength, stamina, and body control. He could also hold his breath for a year! One time Adriana got her tether line tangled up in a stand of sea fans. In the process of cutting herself free, she accidentally sliced through her air hose. Now she had to "buddy breathe" to rise to the surface — with her partner, Kaz, sharing his regulator.

It was a tense moment for any diver, but Kaz remained calm, just as he had in the German bomber. Star watched the ascent anxiously, ready to offer help. None had been required. From what she could tell, Kaz barely needed more than a breath or two on the way up. How would some rink rat learn to do that?

The one thing that Kaz could not seem to get used to was sharks. With the water acting as a magnifying glass, even a small reef shark seemed pretty intimidating, with a mouth large enough to bite your hand off. And, of course, there was still an eighteen-foot tiger shark around somewhere — unless that whole Clarence story was a goof cooked up by Vanover to pull everybody's chain.

Some goof, Kaz thought to himself. He liked the captain. Around Poseidon, Vanover was the only person who seemed to take the summer interns seriously, except maybe Marina.

But Bobby Kaczinski didn't find sharks very funny.

The teen divers took off every fourth day to outgas — to let their systems expel residual nitrogen. It gave them a chance to get to know one another above sea level. The strange turns their internship program had taken seemed to have forced the four closer together. It was something that might never have happened if the summer had gone off as planned.

The institute had mountain bikes for them to borrow, so they explored Saint-Luc's other villages and swam at the many beaches and coves that ringed the small island. Even off the reef they spent much of their time in the water. It was the only way to beat the relentless heat.

Star was awkward on the bicycle at first, until Kaz suggested that the others slow down so she could keep up. Then, somehow, the girl with the limp put on a burst of speed that nearly flattened him. They spent the hours that followed panting to keep up with her on the dirt roads.

"Now I know how to get something done around here," commented Kaz. "Just tell Star she can't do it."

"Maybe we should dare her to air-condition the island," gasped Dante, struggling up a hill at the back of the pack.

As they circled Saint-Luc's west coast, a new skyline began to appear — massive offshore oil-drilling platforms that stretched into the Caribbean like a series of colossal croquet hoops.

"Man," breathed Dante, "look at those."

To see anything man-made in a place as remote as Saint-Luc was jarring. Huge towers of concrete and steel soaring hundreds of feet out of the sea seemed almost fake — clever forgeries merely painted onto the horizon.

"This must be where English works," said Kaz in a small voice. To slip beneath the waves at the feet of such massive pieces of equipment — it was nothing short of terrifying. But for English, it was probably no big deal. The sea did not intimidate Menasce Gérard.

It wouldn't dare.

CHAPTER TEN

Marina Kappas surveyed the light chop that frosted the Caribbean, a frown on her exquisitely formed lips. "It doesn't look too bad on the surface. But I'll bet there's a current a few feet below."

"Yeah, whatever." Star yawned and jumped off the dive platform.

Marina turned to the three remaining interns. "You'll be tethered to the Brownie, but without an anchor line, you can drift without knowing it," she said in concern. "And you'd better watch out for Star. Sometimes confidence can work against you."

Kaz flipped down his own mask. "We'll keep an eye on her." He added quickly, "But don't tell her I said that."

Dante hit the waves with a splash, bit down on his regulator, deflated his B.C., and sank. Sure enough, the current kicked in a few feet below the surface. The unseen force was subtler than wind. And yet it was relentless, propelling him slowly but irresistibly backward.

Don't panic, he told himself, remembering his certification training. *Just keep descending.*

The advice turned out to be correct. By thirty feet, the manhandling of the ocean began to weaken. That was when he noticed something unusual.

Where are all the fish?

The reef was empty. The coral was still there — with its growth of anemones and sea fans. But the permanent traffic jam of fish that characterized the Hidden Shoals was just plain gone.

He shot a questioning look at Adriana. His partner shrugged, mystified.

The disturbance came from above. At first, it seemed like portable rapids — a fast-moving wave of violently foaming water.

He tried to swing his camera around to get a shot of the phenomenon, but he spun too hard, twirling himself on a diagonal axis like a globe. Peering through the lens of the Nikonos, he saw a blurry panorama, and then —

Two eyes and a protruding snout staring right back at him!

He nearly jumped out of his wet suit. Then he recognized the creature in front of him.

A dolphin!

A whole pod of them, in fact, scouring the

reef in a cacophony of high-pitched squeals and clicks. Dante tried to guess at their number, but the sea mammals were moving too fast — faster, in fact, than he'd ever seen anything travel in water. There were at least twenty of them, maybe thirty, diving and swooping as they streaked past.

His visitor circled him with a lightning spin-o-rama, and darted off to join the group.

No wonder the fish cleared out. This is a hunting party. They're not gone; they're hiding!

He began shooting pictures. Dante had seen dolphins only at aquariums and theme parks. These appeared similar — Atlantic bottlenoses. But the show tanks of Sea World could not begin to demonstrate the *personality* of these animals. Fish eyes were blank and staring. But the expression of a dolphin sparkled with charisma, even humor. The face that had scared Dante out of his wits wasn't a threatening one. On the contrary, it had been almost mocking, as if to say, "Man, you're a lousy swimmer. What are you doing in my ocean?"

I need a video camera, he thought to himself. Still pictures would never do justice to the dolphins' playfulness. He squinted at a small dark object that appeared to be swimming along with the pod. It was a conch shell, batted from snout to snout. A toy!

They're practically people! He wondered whether the dolphins would consider that a compliment.

A practiced bump from a bottlenose floated the shell directly into Kaz's hands. The boy lobbed it back into the pack only to have it expertly volleyed to Adriana.

They're not just playing, Dante marveled. *They're playing with us!*

The game lasted maybe thirty seconds before Dante bobbled and dropped the shell, earning a squeaky reprimand from a five-foot cetacean. To interact with these creatures, so alien yet so strangely human, was something he would never forget.

But Star was not ready to say good-bye to their new friends. With a Herculean double kick of her flippers, she came up behind a dorsal fin and latched on to it. The dolphin seemed surprised at first, and then sped up, carrying the girl along for the ride. Suddenly, Dante felt his safety line go taut. And then he was flying through the water at spectacular velocity.

Shock soon turned to amazement. Since the four divers were connected via the Brownie, Star's dolphin was towing them all! He could see Kaz and Adriana, sailing along with him. Kaz's arms were spread like airplane wings. Those maniacs were *enjoying* this!

Like it's some kind of underwater roller coaster.

The other dolphins kept pace with them as the reef accelerated to a blur.

But is it safe?

Dante never saw the coral head swinging out to meet him.

CHAPTER ELEVEN

Wham!

Dante bounced off the tower of living lime-stone like a rag doll. The jolt halted the Brownie on the surface, and yanked Star off her purchase on the dolphin. The ride was over. The streaking pod disappeared from view a few seconds later.

The divers gathered around Dante, who hung in the water, dazed but unhurt, the Nikonos dangling limply from its arm harness.

Star peered into his mask, fearing that the collision had knocked him unconscious. But his eyes were open and alert, fixed on the seafloor.

For Dante, it was like studying a pixelgram — that moment when your brain makes the connection, and you plunge into the depths of 3-D. It wasn't even a real image — more like the echo of one, formed by thousands of layers of coral polyps growing over an object long buried, long forgotten.

He deflated his B.C. and began to descend to the bottom. The others followed, confused. They didn't see it, *couldn't* see it.

THE DISCOVERY

In his excitement, he nearly fumbled away his dive slate. He scribbled the word that was pounding in his brain, revving his heartbeat up to the danger zone:

ANCHOR.

They stared at him blankly.

What are you, blind? he wanted to howl. *Right there — in front of your noses!*

The same condition that held color tantalizingly out of his grasp revealed the presence of the anchor in the subtleties of light and texture and shading. The others would never see it. He had to *show* them.

But how? Coral was like rock; it was rock beneath the living layers at the surface.

A few feet away, the reef gave way to sandy bottom. He began to dig, burrowing with both hands. Instantly, the crystal-clear water was murky with mud and silt.

Star, Kaz, and Adriana watched him, their bewilderment evident. Had Dante's collision scrambled his brain? Why was he using the ocean floor as a sandbox?

Kaz touched his arm, but Dante shook it away. He was a man on a mission, tunneling down to the lost anchor. *How big do they make these things? If the top is long enough, then it should be right about —*

His glove struck something hard. "Got it!" he cried into his regulator.

He had stirred up so much silt that the sea was churning brown. He took Kaz's gloved hand and pressed it against ancient iron.

Star removed a fin and fanned the water clear above the buried object. They could make out part of a thick shank topped with a sturdy ring. A small black disk floated beside it, disturbed by the digging action.

A chip off the old metal?

Dante stuck it in his dive pouch — proof of the anchor's existence. But there was another problem: How would they ever find this spot again?

Then he remembered the marker buoys. He clipped one around the iron ring, and sent the balloon shooting for the surface. They followed it up, carefully matching the pace of the slowest of their bubbles.

A few bold fish watched them ascend — the advance scouts venturing out of hiding to make sure the dolphins were gone. The reef was returning to normal.

The divers broke into the chop and swam a short distance to the Brownie. The *Ponce de León* was almost upon them, a silhouette against the brilliant sun.

"Over here!" panted Star, waving her arms.

THE DISCOVERY

"We found something!" added Dante.

Marina jumped down to the dive platform to help them aboard. "I don't see a lot of markers."

"Not a cave," Dante exclaimed. "An anchor!"

"You're kidding!" Cutter came running, Reardon hot on his heels. Soon the four divers stood dripping on deck.

Adriana pulled off her flippers. "Is that what you're looking for? With the magnetometer?" She added, "We know you're not taking sonar readings."

The three scientists exchanged a meaningful look. Finally, Marina spoke. "Our tow fish can do both — side scan mag and sonar. When we publish our map, it's going to come with an overlay page of mineral deposits under the reef. That's what the mag is for."

"What about this anchor?" Reardon put in gruffly.

"Dante found it," Kaz explained breathlessly. "Most of it's buried in coral. You can tell it's really old."

"I got a piece of it," added Dante, fumbling in his pouch.

Cutter frowned. "A piece of anchor?"

"More like a chip." The photographer pulled out the small black disk. It was irregular in shape, but generally round, about three inches in diameter. "Is there some way to get it analyzed? You know, find out how old it is?"

A gasp escaped Reardon, which Marina extinguished with a stern look.

Cutter spoke up carefully. "I'm telling you this now, because I know how embarrassed you were when word got around the institute about that German plane. Guys, you just found the anchor of the *Queen Anne's Revenge*."

Adriana gawked at him. "*Blackbeard's* ship?"

"Don't you remember the movie? Harrison Ford played the diver who spotted the anchor buried in the mud."

"You're not saying — " Star's eyes narrowed. "Another film prop?"

Cutter nodded. "It took the location people three weeks to plant it deep enough on the bottom."

"That anchor wasn't in mud," Kaz pointed out. "It was in coral."

"Coral grows fast," put in Marina. "Especially on something hard like an anchor. How old is that movie — seven or eight years?"

"But the *Queen Anne's Revenge* didn't sink in the Caribbean," Adriana pointed out. "It went aground off the Carolinas. Why shoot the film here?"

THE DISCOVERY

Cutter shrugged. "On-screen, water is water. You can't tell the latitude by looking at it. Hollywood people like to work where the sea's nice and warm and crystal clear. It's easier and cheaper."

Dante regarded his anchor chip with chagrin. "Worthless." As he reared back to pitch the black disk into the sea, Reardon bulled forward and snatched it out of his hand. "Mind if I hang on to this?" he asked. "I'm a big Harrison Ford fan."

Star looked disgusted. "Is there anything else we should know about before we make total idiots out of ourselves? Did Steven Spielberg recreate the lost continent of Atlantis over by the oil rigs?"

Marina laughed. "Don't be embarrassed. You kids are doing beautifully, and you're turning into top-notch divers. Don't let yourselves get obsessed with sunken anchors or crazy discoveries. You'll just end up disappointed."

"Right," agreed Cutter. "Anything of value in these waters has been salvaged decades ago. There's nothing left to find down there."

Throughout the conversation, Chris Reardon did not take his eyes off the small black disk.

11 August 1665

The Griffin's store of fruit had long since gone rotten, and was maggot infested besides.

"Eat it, young Samuel," ordered York, the ship's barber. "The maggots too. They'll keep the teeth in your head."

Samuel closed his eyes and took a tiny bite of the moldy apple. He could feel the wormy insects moving on his tongue, and quickly swallowed, choking back his nausea.

As barber, York was in charge of much more than cutting hair. He was the Griffin's sole medical man, apothecary, and dentist.

"Scurvy takes the teeth first," he lectured. "Then the mind. Then your life."

It was true. At the start of the crossing, each crewman aboard the ship had been allotted a small quantity of fruit. Those who had not jealously hoarded their shares were now suffering deeply from the disease. Toothless, their bodies bent from pain, they stumbled around the barque, struggling to perform their duties. Many more had given up trying, and hung in their berths, eyes wide with vacant stares. Of two and eighty seamen and four and thirty Viscount survivors, only sixty men — barely half — remained. Now, nearly four months out of England, the rest had succumbed to scurvy, fever, and the relentless assault of the Atlantic. The gut-wrenching stink of death joined the mix of overpowering smells that made up the reek of the ship.

The funerals were becoming commonplace — two or three a day now. Normally, a body would be wrapped in a shroud for burial at sea. But sewing the shrouds was the office of the sail maker, and Evans was long gone. Samuel was struggling to take over the old man's duties, but it was all he could do to keep the Griffin's patchwork canvas aloft. So the dead were dispatched naked to their final resting places.

"It makes no difference to the sharks," was Captain Blade's opinion. "A meal's a meal, wrapped or no."

The cruel seaman never missed a flogging, yet never attended a single funeral. "A captain has more important things on his plate than feeding fish," he told Samuel.

An hour did not pass in which Samuel neglected to curse himself for saving his master's life on the ratlines. His hatred of the captain grew stronger, not weaker, as the barque approached the New World.

But even as resentment swelled inside Samuel,

James Blade had begun to warm to the cabin boy who had stopped his fall that fateful day.

On the surface, there was no difference. The captain continued to treat him as a slave who was unworthy of even the slightest consideration. But it was Blade who had ordered the barber to keep an eye out for the young seaman the crew now called Lucky.

Never mind that the men of the Griffin avoided York like an evil spirit. He was most often seen covered in gore, sawing an unfortunate sailor's leg off. His newfound "friendship" with Samuel only served to make the boy feel like even more of an outcast. And he had James Blade to thank for it.

Samuel's feelings for the captain were not helped by the information he acquired on bailing duty in the ship's bilge. As he battled the pumps and the stench, he overheard some sailors chortling over the day when the hold would be piled high with gold and silver. Soon, they said, the Griffin would wallow low in the water from a cargo of plundered Spanish treasure, and all aboard her would be rich.

Samuel pounded back to the captain's quarters as soon as his shift was over, ignoring fatigue and the cramping of his muscles. He found Blade at the small desk, examining his rutter — the secret diary of a ship's pilot who had sailed this route before. No map, no chart, no instrument was as vital to a safe voyage as a good rutter.

"Sir!" he cried. Distraught, he related what he had heard from the pumpers in the hold. "It can't be so, can it, Captain? Tell me we're not — common pirates!"

"Pirates?!" The bone handle of the snake whip came down on Samuel's head with devastating, murderous force. The last thing he saw before the captain's cabin went dark was James Blade, his cheeks suffused with purple rage.

Samuel awoke to a stinging pain so great it seared his very soul. He was in the barber's surgery. York was pouring seawater over a bloody gash on the boy's crown.

"A friendly piece of advice, young Samuel," the man said, a trace of humor in his voice. "Never say 'pirate' to Captain Blade. A right good thing it is that he's taken a liking to you."

Samuel tried to sit up, but the torment was too much. "We are pirates," he mumbled bitterly. "Thieves. Murderers too, probably."

"Listen to me, boy," York ordered. "We're patriots, with the full backing of the king of England. There are papers on board signed by the Merry Monarch himself in proper London. They give us the right — no, the responsibility — to attack and disrupt enemy shipping in the Indies."

Samuel frowned. "How does it help England if we steal their treasure?"

"Gold buys ships, boy. And trains soldiers, and equips them with muskets and cannon," the barber explained. "We're at war, Lucky, and wealth is power. The Royal Navy can't waste a ship on every stinking fever-hole in the New World. That's our lot — the patriots, the privateers! We're legal as a magistrate, flush with letters of marque to raid the scurvy Dutch."

"But — " Samuel was confused. "But they were talking about Spanish treasure, not Dutch."

"True that is," York agreed. "And a beastly nuisance to us that His Majesty, God bless him, called a truce with the cursed Spaniard. But the ocean is large, and the courtly affairs of Europe far distant. Mistakes are made, you see my point? A Spanish ship looks much like a Dutch ship in the heat of battle, and treasure is treasure, no matter whose dead hand you pry it from."

He put an arm around the cabin boy's shoulders, and Samuel winced from the stench of decay on his blood-spattered smock. The barber's pockmarked face was barely an inch from his own, his breath as foul as the rest of him. "And in this part of the world, Lucky, no treasure shines as bright as Spanish gold."

THE DISCOVERY

CHAPTER TWELVE

Kaz stumbled through the darkness of 4:45 A.M. along the boardwalk that connected the Poseidon compound to the small marina. There was little moon. Only a handful of stars flickered through the overcast to light his way.

A dull clunk — his dive bag, falling to the dock. As he bent down, groping through the gloom, his knife slipped from its scabbard and planted itself with a *boing* tip first in the weathered planking. It could just as easily have been in Kaz's foot.

With a groan that was overwhelmed by a yawn, he gathered up his gear. Hockey players lugged a lot of equipment too. Why was he so discombobulated this morning?

"Kaz! That you?"

Dante beckoned from the harbor lights. Kaz gathered up his things and hurried over. "Where's the boat?"

"Gone," the boy told him.

"You're kidding!" Squinting, he took inventory of the various research vessels and launches that

DIVE

bobbed by the dock. There was no *Ponce de León*.

"Maybe it's in for service," suggested Dante. "Like, change the oil — "

"Rotate the tires," Kaz added sarcastically.

"You know what I mean. Boat stuff."

"What boat stuff?" Star came into the light, her dive bag draped over her shoulder.

Adriana was right behind her. She did a quick scan of the harbor. "Not again. I thought all this was behind us."

"It could be a maintenance problem," put in Dante.

"Yeah, well, I want to hear that from Cutter." Star dumped her gear on the dock and marched back up the boardwalk toward the institute. Her limp added an ill-fitting wobble to her almost military gait, but the others followed without comment. All too well they recognized the look of determination on the slight girl's face.

Only Kaz ventured a discouraging word. "You know, if the boat's being serviced, Cutter's probably grabbing some extra sleep."

"I don't care if he's in a coma." Star strode purposefully up to the small cabin and rapped on the door.

The team leader wasn't home, so they tried

the main lab area, where Cutter, Marina, and Reardon shared a small office.

"Tad?" The door was slightly ajar. Star pushed it open and turned on the light.

The room was deserted, the desk hidden under piles of maps and data printouts. The only other object on it was a drinking glass filled with what appeared to be water. In the bottom sat a small metal disk.

"Blackbeard's anchor," said Dante sarcastically. "Coming soon to a theater near you." But when he took a step toward it, he noticed a sharp chemical smell coming from the clear liquid. And when he peered into the glass itself, he saw that his artifact had *changed*.

The strong solution had eaten away the black coating. Now the piece gleamed shiny silver. Even more amazing, the thing was stamped with a design — a worn pattern, perhaps a coat of arms.

Dante was thunderstruck. This wasn't part of the anchor at all. It was a co*in*!

He turned to the others. "Guys — is that what I think it is?"

Kaz peered into the glass. "Silver, right?"

"Definitely," said Star. "It's pretty crude, but I guarantee that's some kind of money."

Adriana stepped forward, eyes alight. "Not just money. That's a piece of eight!"

Dante stared at her. "A piece of *what*?"

"Spanish money," she explained excitedly. "From hundreds of years ago! They have lots of it at the British Museum. In the seventeenth century, this silver piece was the most common coin in the world. Eight reals — a piece of eight."

Dante perked up. "Is it worth anything?"

"What do you think?" Star asked sarcastically. "It's a three-hundred-year-old coin."

"It's living history," Adriana amended. "This coin was made from silver pulled out of the mines of South America by descendants of the Incas. You can't put a price on that."

"Fifty bucks?" prompted Dante. "A hundred? More? Man, I almost chucked it overboard!"

Kaz's eyes narrowed. "But Reardon wouldn't let you. He practically leaped across the boat to get it off you."

"He knew," Star agreed bitterly. "And so did Cutter. That anchor wasn't any movie prop. We found something, and they're trying to steal it from us."

"We'll steal it back!" Dante decided.

"Brilliant," approved Kaz. "And what about the anchor down there? You can't just hide that in your underwear drawer. We have to get it on official record that this find is *ours*. Let's go to Gallagher."

When Dr. Geoffrey Gallagher arrived at his office promptly at eight that morning, he found the four teenage interns fast asleep on his doorstep.

"Good morning," he said loudly enough to startle them awake. He noticed with some annoyance that his cameraman was filming the four as they scrambled to their feet.

Kaz found his voice first. "Dr. Gallagher, we have a problem. We found this coin — "

"A Spanish piece of eight — " Adriana put in.

"An anchor too," added Dante. "I spotted it first. I thought it broke off the anchor, but it turned out to be a coin — "

Star cut him off. "But Chris Reardon stole it — "

"Well, we gave it away," Kaz took up the narrative, "but we didn't know it was a coin then. We thought it was part of a movie prop — "

It was the truth, but it was coming out in a scattered jumble of half sentences and interruptions as the groggy four struggled to give voice to their disorganized thoughts.

Gallagher grimaced in perplexity. At least, he noted, the cameraman had stopped filming these babbling youngsters. It was obvious that they had nothing to add to a scientific documentary.

He pulled himself up to his full six feet. "What you young interns don't seem to understand is that this institute is actually dozens of independent projects, headed by dozens of different scientists. I make it possible for these projects to function, but I have no authority within the projects themselves."

They looked blank, so he simplified his language. "Your boss is Mr. Cutter, not me. If you have anything to report, you report it to him."

"But that's the whole problem — " Kaz began.

At that moment, Dr. Gallagher noticed that the camera's red light was on again. He gave his most public smile. "You young people are the future of the oceanographic community. You are an asset to Poseidon."

And he and his cameraman entered the office, shutting the door in their faces.

Angrily, Kaz reached for the handle.

"Forget it," grumbled Star. "The guy's a dolt. All he cares about is looking good on video."

Discouraged, they straggled back to the dock to retrieve their diving gear.

Dante sat down on a weathered piling. "Some summer this turned out to be," he growled. "I feel like getting on the next catamaran to Martinique and the first flight home. I should tell them to stick their internship. It's not like I'm pumping out thousands of great pictures."

"I'd leave too," Adriana said quietly, "but there's nowhere to go. My parents are in Saint-Tropez or Corfu or wherever the in place is to go this year."

Star folded her arms in front of her. "I'm not a quitter."

"None of us are quitters," Kaz retorted. "We're just talking, okay? Don't tell me you're not disappointed with how this internship's been going."

"I should be the most disappointed of anybody," grumbled Dante. "Technically, that's *my* coin they ripped off. I'm the one who found the anchor."

Star looked at him curiously. "There's another thing I've been wondering about. How did you see that? And you spotted the plane too. How come you see things other people don't?"

Dante looked away. "Maybe I have better eyesight than the rest of you guys."

"You've got terrible eyesight," Adriana put in. "You think the ocean is purple."

"No, I don't," the photographer defended himself. "That was a darkroom error."

"Or those scuba tanks," Kaz persisted. "You thought a red sticker was a green sticker."

"I got confused — " Dante managed weakly.

"Between red and green?"

When it finally came out, it cascaded from him in an avalanche. "Don't you get it? To me, red is green, and green is red, and they're both gray! I'm color-blind! The great photographic prodigy is living inside a black-and-white movie!"

The others were stunned.

Kaz was first to find his voice. "How does that help you pick out an anchor buried in coral?"

"You guys look at a reef and see a billion different colors. But to me, it's all a super-detailed charcoal sketch. I focus on shading and texture, rough and smooth, raised and flat. To you, that anchor was invisible. But to me, the shape under the coral was as obvious as a person under a blanket. I couldn't see it directly, but I knew it was there."

Adriana spoke up. "But why would you take color pictures if you can't see color? How could you ever hope to get it right?"

Dante shrugged unhappily. "I don't know. I guess I figured I could learn to fake it or something — connect certain shading to certain colors. But it's no use. Some handicap for a photographer, huh?"

THE DISCOVERY

"That's not a handicap," Star said sharply. "That's a *gift*. You see what other people can't. Poor you."

As they sat on the dock, feeling sorry for themselves, the sound of an approaching engine caught their attention. It was the *Hernando Cortés*, with Captain Vanover at the wheel. He tooted the horn twice and waved at them.

Adriana raised an eyebrow. "You know," she began thoughtfully, "Gallagher won't listen to us, but what about the captain? He always takes us seriously. Maybe we should tell *him* about the coin."

"And maybe he'll steal it from off Cutter so he can keep it for himself," Dante put in cynically. "Vanover's nice, but so is Marina. And she lies to our faces. Who knows who you can trust around here?"

"Agreed," said Kaz. "This is between us and Cutter. We'll keep it to ourselves."

The *Cortés* moved smoothly into its berth, and the hulking figure of Menasce Gérard leaped over the gunwale and tied up the vessel. He did not look in their direction, and they were not sorry.

Vanover called to them from the cockpit. "Morning, guys." He noticed their diving equipment piled up on the dock, noted the absence of the *Ponce de León*, and looked disgusted. "Not again."

Kaz nodded. "They stood us up. We were here by five. They were already gone."

"That tears it! Load up your gear and get on board. I'll take you to Cutter."

When English came back from the harbormaster's office, he was dismayed to find the four teens aboard, and Vanover preparing to cast off.

The dive guide was annoyed. "Captain, *pourquoi* — why these teenagers again?"

"Relax, English," the captain soothed. "We're just a taxi service. Cutter blew them off, and I'm not going to let him get away with it this time."

English looked suspicious. "No diving?"

"Not with us," Vanover promised. "We'll radio the office and get the *Ponce's* location. There and back, that's all."

CHAPTER THIRTEEN

The *Cortés* was seven miles out of Côte Saint-Luc when they heard the blast.

"Thunder?" asked Dante. There wasn't a cloud in the sky.

Vanover and English exchanged a look, and the captain cranked up the boat's speed. On the open water, a boom like that usually meant an engine explosion.

English took over the helm, and Vanover rushed belowdecks to the radio. "This is the *Cortés* calling the *Ponce*. Bill, we just heard a whale of a bang. Are you and your people all right?"

There was no answer. The captain repeated the message. Still nothing.

English leaned on the throttle, and the research vessel surged ahead.

The four young divers braced against bulwarks as the chop tossed the racing boat. Their expressions were sober. Had something happened to Cutter and his crew?

At last, the *Ponce de León* appeared, a speck on the horizon.

Vanover studied it through binoculars. "Well,

it's in one piece," he reported. "And I don't see any fire."

English maintained top velocity. "And the people?"

"Nobody yet," said the captain.

They were four hundred yards off the other vessel's starboard bow when the radio crackled to life. Bill Hamilton, captain of the *Ponce de León*. "This is the *Ponce*. Braden, is that you?"

"What's going on, Bill? Is everybody okay over there? Why didn't you answer our hail?"

Tad Cutter's voice came on the line. "Things got kind of crazy around here. You wouldn't believe the engine backfire we just had."

"That was a backfire?" Vanover exclaimed. "It sounded like a bomb!"

"We're checking the engine now," Cutter went on. "But I'm pretty sure we're all right. Thanks anyway, Braden."

"Not so fast," said the captain. "I've got a surprise for you, Cutter. Four surprises, actually. You left a little something on the dock this morning."

"Oh, yeah, the kids. We got an early start today. I didn't have the heart to wake them."

"Yeah, well, they're awake now. And they're coming over."

"Not a good idea," Cutter warned. "My compressor's down, so they can't dive."

"No problem," Vanover assured him. "I've got a few charged scuba tanks. We'll come alongside, put them in the water from our platform, and they'll ride home with you when you're done."

There was a very long silence. Then, "Sounds like a plan."

By this time, the two boats were close enough together that Kaz could see Cutter, Marina, and Reardon on the deck of the *Ponce de León*. Reardon was in the stern, checking the fishing line that seemed to be his foremost concern aboard the research vessel. If Kaz had not been preoccupied with struggling into his tropical suit, he might have noticed that Reardon's hair was wet. The bearded man had been in the water, and recently.

The *Cortés* idled one hundred feet astern of the *Ponce de León*, and the four divers took to the waves.

"Remember" — Vanover's parting words — "you have every right to be here. You didn't pick Poseidon; Poseidon picked you. Don't be afraid to tell that to Cutter."

Floating on the surface, Star muttered, "There are plenty of things I intend to tell Cutter."

"What's the point?" sneered Kaz, treading water. "He lied to us before; he'll lie to us again."

"Hi, guys!" Marina beckoned from the deck

of the *Ponce de León*, beaming and waving. "Come aboard! We're moving off!"

"In your dreams," muttered Star. "I'm going down to see what they've been up to." She flipped her mask over her nose and mouth. "Who's with me?"

"Me," volunteered Adriana.

"But what are we supposed to tell Marina?" asked Dante.

"Tell her we didn't hear," Star said. "Her voice doesn't carry so good. I might never hear her again." She bit down on her regulator, deflated her B.C., and disappeared below the surface. Adriana followed.

The water was dark and murky — almost opaque. What had happened to the clear blue Caribbean?

As Star continued to descend, she kept one eye on the fluid kick of Adriana's flippers slightly above her. It would be easy to lose track of her partner in this silt.

Silt. That's what it was. But what force could stir up so much of the stuff? An engine backfire? Not likely.

Forty feet. Where was the bottom?

A curious barracuda peered at them through the pea soup and darted quickly away.

Sixty feet. How deep was it here? The visibility was so bad it was impossible to tell. There was almost no light now. Star felt isolated, disoriented. Only the direction of her bubbles told her which way was up.

Suddenly, her flippers scraped something unseen. The reef! She valved air into her B.C. to make herself neutrally buoyant, and grabbed Adriana before the girl hit bottom. The two squinted at each other in the gloom. Cutter and company may well have been up to something, but the girls weren't likely to find evidence of it with the ocean in this condition.

They swam along the seafloor, following the line of the reef from a few feet above it. And then, quite abruptly, the coral spine was no longer there.

Star gawked. This was no natural feature. It was almost like a crater in the reef — a circular zone maybe a dozen feet in diameter.

She finned ahead and peered down. The hole was filled with chunks of broken coral of all sizes, from boulders to gravel.

The realization almost took her breath away. Cutter's "backfire" — dynamite! An explosion big enough to break the coral and send clouds of muck and silt billowing in all directions!

Her initial reaction was outrage, followed quickly by bewilderment. Why would a bunch of oceanographers — scientists! — dynamite a living reef? This detonation meant the deaths of tens of millions of polyps, an environmental disaster that would take decades to regenerate. It wasn't just despicable; it was illegal! Coral was protected around the world.

But mostly, it flat-out made no sense. What was to be gained by such mindless destruction?

All at once, the shape came together, a familiar image concealed by the rubble that had been the reef. A dark form amid the lighter, multicolored debris: a ring, cross, and double hook — Dante's anchor. The marker buoy had been removed, but there was no question it was the same artifact.

They're after our discovery!

Star felt a pinch on the sleeve of her wet suit. Adriana, coming to the same conclusion.

Everything fell into place. No scientist would dynamite coral. But Tad Cutter was no scientist. It explained the magnetometer, and why Cutter kept his interns busy tagging caves when he took them out at all.

And it explained why he and his people had instantly recognized the Spanish coin for what it was.

Cutter, Marina, and Reardon may have worked for Poseidon, but they were treasure hunters!

A sweep of Adriana's flipper stirred up the pebbles of shattered coral below them. Star caught sight of something else in the swirl of movement — something smooth rather than jagged, and stark white. She reached into the debris and picked it up — a hilt or handle, perhaps eight inches long. It was carved and polished — and definitely man-made.

A meaningful look passed between the two scuba masks. Had Dante and his sharp eyes inadvertently led Cutter and his team to exactly what they were looking for?

CHAPTER FOURTEEN

It was the first time Kaz had ever seen Marina Kappas angry.

"They had no right to dive! I ordered them aboard!"

"We couldn't hear you," Kaz called up to the *Ponce de León*.

"I want them *now!*" she exploded. "You go down there and get them. We have a schedule to keep."

Kaz dipped his face mask in the water and popped right up again. "Cloudy today. Let's go down the anchor line. It'll be easier to stay together."

He and Dante began to kick their way around the stern of the boat.

"Hurry!" Marina exclaimed peevishly. "We don't have all day!"

A sharp ringing buzz cut the air. It took Kaz a few seconds to identify the sound — Chris Reardon's unmanned fishing reel, playing out at light speed. Reardon's special bait, squid parts mixed with cold pizza, had hooked something big.

It happened before Kaz could even bite down

on his mouthpiece. The thousand-pound Mylar line wrapped around him, pinning his right arm to his body. He was dragged below the surface, keenly aware of a force many times his own strength.

Fighting off panic, he used his free hand to fumble his regulator into his mouth. He squinted through the murky water and got a bead on the dark shape at the end of the line. It was a huge grouper, four hundred pounds or more, hooked and fighting wildly. In the creature's mad struggle for its life, it was pulling Kaz straight for the bottom, its desperate gyrations tugging the Mylar ever tighter around the helpless diver.

I'll never fight it, he thought, the water rushing past him, the big fish just a blur. *My only hope is to cut myself free.*

His dive knife was in a scabbard on his right thigh. He could just reach it with his left hand. As his glove closed over the hilt, the big grouper abruptly changed direction. Kaz was yanked after it like a puppy on a leash. In agony, he felt the knife slip through his fingers. His last hope, swallowed by the churning sea.

No, he reminded himself. *There's still one chance. Something has to stop that grouper.*

And something did. At first, Kaz thought it was a submarine — it had to be, something so big. But then the huge torpedo-like shape opened a gaping mouth. And when it snapped shut, half the grouper was gone.

The Mylar line went slack, but Kaz made no attempt to shrug himself loose. He was paralyzed with a fear that dated back to his very early childhood. For he knew, as surely as if the big fish had been wearing a neon name tag, that this was the eighteen-foot monster tiger shark the locals called Clarence.

Still sinking slowly, he watched the enormous jaws savage the grouper in a cloud of blood and tattered flesh. The blood looked green at this depth. *The color red is filtered out by seawater.* . . . His scuba instructor's voice echoed in his head, repeating the words in an endless loop. Kaz was powerless to stop the lecture. His mind had shut down. Terror was in charge.

He had left home, family, hockey, everything that was familiar, to travel two thousand miles to the Caribbean — to die.

He barely noticed the moment that he bumped into the seabed. It was almost a comfort. A place to hide while the big shark circled overhead, snapping violently at the bloody scraps around it. To Clarence, blood in the water meant food. The predator already had no memory of the grouper it had just devoured. It never gave a thought to its last meal; its next one was the main concern.

Kaz huddled on the sandy bottom, trembling with dread. No plan was taking shape in his mind, no strategy for survival. Even the inescapable fact that his air supply wouldn't last forever could not penetrate his overpowering compulsion to hide from nature's perfect killing machine.

Dante broke the surface and spit out his regulator, gasping in the fresh air.

"Shark!" he tried to yell. It came out a high-pitched wheeze.

He looked around desperately. He was closer to the *Ponce de León* than the *Cortés*, but he instinctively began thrashing toward Vanover's boat. When it was a matter of life and death, you went with the people you trusted.

Something bubbled up out of the water directly in his path, and he screamed in shock and fear.

Star pushed her mask aside. "Not so loud," she warned. "Listen, we found out what Cutter's — "

"*Clarence!*" Dante bellowed right in her face.

"Who?"

"The shark!"

Adriana hit the surface, and this time both Dante and Star recoiled.

"Where's Kaz?" Star asked.

"He's on the bottom and he's not moving!" Dante wailed. "I couldn't get to him! The shark — "

Star was already kicking for the *Cortés*, shouting, "*Captain!*"

Both Vanover and English were on the dive platform to pull the three out of the water.

"What's going on?" the captain demanded. "Where's Kaz?"

Chest heaving, Dante sobbed out a breathless explanation. "The shark didn't bite him," he babbled on, "but I think he's too scared to come up!"

English was already strapping on a scuba tank.

"It sounds like old Clarence," Vanover decided. "You'd better take the shark cage."

The dive guide scowled. "I am not a canary, me."

"The kid could be injured, even bleeding," Vanover argued. "You'll need the cage because of him."

English grunted his agreement.

They spent precious minutes unfolding the titanium cage and attaching it to the *Cortés*'s electric winch. English climbed inside and pulled the door shut. The clang sounded like the closing of a prison cell.

Vanover swung the cage over the gunwale. "One tug for down, two for up, three for stop." He hit the winch, and the guide disappeared into the sea.

Menasce Gérard was as much at home in the ocean as on land. In his commercial work with the oil rigs, he often descended to depths of a thousand feet or more — thirty atmospheres of pressure. He feared nothing down here and viewed the cage as an inconvenience, almost an embarrassment. Why was he surprised that those American teenagers had brought him to this?

The poor visibility was unexpected. But, alors, this made perfect sense. No single shark could disturb so much silt. But whatever had done it might very well attract a large predator like Clarence.

He peered through the bars, looking for the shark and the young diver, but there was no sign of either. When the cage hit bottom, he gave a triple yank on the signal rope, the sign for stop. Then he opened the steel door and ventured out.

He had no weight belt, so maintaining depth was a struggle. He could do it, but not forever, and the effort would surely deplete his air supply quickly. He had to find Kaz right now.

The cloudy water made the search difficult. The minutes fell away. How many? Even a veteran diver couldn't judge. Too many.

He passed directly over the boy and almost missed him in the gloom. Kaz lay flat against the sand as if attempting to bury himself in it. At first, English mistook the blackness of the boy's wet suit for a large sea fan that had fallen over.

Kaz nearly jumped out of his skin when the dive guide grabbed him under the arms and pulled him upright.

Menasce Gérard did not waste words anywhere, especially underwater. "Come," he said into his regulator.

Kaz grabbed the big man's arm and did not let go. Now connected to a weighted diver, English was able to lead the way efficiently along the bottom toward the cage.

It might have been underwater radar, or even a sixth sense, but English knew instantly when the shark began pursuing them. A quick glance over his shoulder revealed nothing. But the predator was coming, concealed by the swirling silt. English could picture the eighteen-foot monster with the cold black eyes.

He spit out another word: "Faster." He still couldn't see Clarence, but he was aware of a dark shape behind them, and it was growing larger. They kicked like machines, propelling themselves toward the cage and safety.

Kaz did not risk a look back, but there was horror behind his mask, and the desperation of the hunted.

The shadows ahead began to resolve themselves into the straight lines and right angles of the cage. But the shark was visible too now, and gaining. Its sweeping tail powered the attack as it closed the gap, mouth slightly open, lethal arsenal at the ready.

With a burst of speed and strength that surprised even him, English finned for the cage and thrust Kaz inside. He scrambled in himself, and grabbed the door to swing it shut.

And then the great mouth exploded out of the shadowy deep with appalling violence.

CHAPTER FIFTEEN

Jaws the size of a small desk clamped down on the bars of the still-open door in a shriek of bone on metal. The powerful head began to shake relentlessly. The cage tossed, its occupants rattling around like backgammon dice in a cup.

The tugging from the struggle must have reached the surface, because the cage began to rise. The shark remained clamped on the gate, stubbornly trying to bite through the two-inch titanium. English braced himself against the rear slats, kicking frantically with his flippers at the flat blunt snout.

Hanging on to the bars to avoid being catapulted out the opening, Kaz knew a panic he would not have imagined possible. He saw that the only thing keeping them alive at this point was the tiger shark's own stupidity. For if the beast had the sense to let go of the door, it would have been able to poke its head inside the cage and reach them.

The glowing dial of his Fathometer watch showed that the surface was still forty feet away.

When the cage rose above the waves, he wondered if he and English would still be in it.

Aboard the *Hernando Cortés*, Captain Vanover bent over his electric winch, which was groaning and vibrating.

Dante looked worried. "Does it do that all the time?"

"Shouldn't," the captain frowned. "Not to reel in a cage and two divers."

Star peered over the stern. "I can't see anything. No, wait — "

The others rushed to join her at the gunwale.

The ocean was boiling, churning up white water from the depths.

Adriana drew in a sharp breath. "Holy — "

The cage broke the surface, and with it rose the tiger shark, a writhing mass of muscle and fury as thick as a redwood. It was still doggedly clamped on to the bars of the door, being winched from the water up past its huge triangular dorsal fin. Now, hoisted out of the element that was its home, the beast went completely berserk, twisting and thrashing as its snapping jaws punished the tempered steel.

Vanover grabbed a long pole and began beating at the shark's enormous head. Star hefted another and jabbed sharply at the white underbelly. Dante bounced a soda can off a pectoral fin. Nothing seemed to have any effect.

Kaz remained cemented to the bars, still breathing out of his regulator, although he hung six feet above the water.

Bellowing French curses, English shrugged out of his scuba harness, reared back with the compressed air tank, and brought it down full force on the shark's obsidian eye. The force of the blow caused the monster to open its vice-grip jaws. It fell back into the sea with a mammoth splash that rocked the boat and sent a torrent of water over the four spectators on deck. It took two menacing laps of the research vessel, its dorsal fin slicing the waves. Then it finally disappeared.

The captain swung the cage over the gunwale and lowered it to the deck.

English hauled Kaz out and yanked the regulator from his mouth. "You are all right, boy? You are in one piece?"

Kaz nodded. His knees felt wobbly, but he was determined not to collapse. "You — you saved my life!"

The dive guide's response was an elaborate shrug that was very French. "But next time," he added pointedly, "you like excitement, you ride the roller coaster, *oui*?"

The radio burst to life in the navigation room belowdecks. Tad Cutter's voice: "What's going on over there? Was that a whale? Is everybody okay?"

Rolling his eyes, Vanover dragged himself down the companionway. "Everybody's fine, Cutter," he said shortly. "One of your interns almost got eaten. Nothing for you to concern yourself about." He severed the connection.

"Hey — " Adriana pointed to the cage. There, pressed into a corner, its skin matching the steel-gray of the bars, cowered a small octopus. "Mr. English — here's the octopus we owe you."

The big guide reached in through the bars, drew out the terrified creature, and spoke directly to it. "You are lucky I'm in a good mood." And he tossed it back into the sea.

It was the only time the four interns had ever seen him smile.

It was decided that the teen divers would ride back to Côte Saint-Luc harbor on the *Hernando Cortés* instead of switching to the *Ponce de León*.

"The last thing you kids need is face time with Cutter and his crew," said Vanover grimly.

Kaz nodded his agreement. "Reardon's probably still sore about losing that grouper. I'll bet he has no idea that his stupid fishing line almost turned me into the catch of the day."

Vanover regarded him seriously. "I've seen too many divers pretend it never happened by making little jokes like that. What you went through — that's as scary as it gets. Here's what you have to decide: Was it a knockout punch? Some guys can shrug off an experience like that and strap on fins the very next morning; others never put a toe in the water again. Your job, Kaz, is to figure out which one you're going to be." He headed up the companionway, leaving them alone in the galley.

"He's right, you know," said Dante. "How are you ever going to be able to dive after today? I don't know if *I* can, and it didn't even happen to me."

"That's just plain dumb," scoffed Star. "Today was a freak accident. Even if you do run into a big shark like that, chances are he'll look right through you and keep on swimming. To quit diving because of this would be like refusing to drive a car because you almost got into an accident once."

"Yeah, but Clarence is still out there somewhere," Dante reminded her.

She shrugged. "The captain says he's been around for years. People hardly ever see him, and even when they do, it's no big deal. Kaz just happened to be there when he was feeding and there was blood in the water."

"Even so — " Dante began.

"I'm still diving," Kaz interrupted suddenly.

Adriana was wary. "You probably shouldn't make up your mind right away."

"I'm still diving," he repeated. The decision had come to him suddenly, unexpectedly. It was something Star said — "a freak accident." How had the doctors described Drew Christiansen's catastrophic injury? *A freak accident. A one in a million shot.* To consider what happened as anything more than pure wild chance was the equivalent of blaming Drew's paralysis on Kaz.

There was no more extra danger of shark attack in these waters than there was likelihood that a body check from Bobby Kaczinski would put another boy in a wheelchair.

The more he thought about it, the more it made sense to him. "Don't worry about me. I'll be fine."

"You're tough, rink rat," Star said with grudging approval.

"Now, listen. You're not going to believe this, but Clarence was not the top news story today."

"That's because it wasn't *your* head he was practically chewing on," Kaz retorted.

"Seriously." Star persisted. "First off, all this didn't happen at some random spot on the reef. We were directly above the anchor back there."

"We saw it," added Adriana. "The whole thing."

"That's impossible!" Dante exclaimed. "It's buried under tons of coral."

"Not anymore." Star informed him, "because Cutter blasted the reef to smithereens. That's why the ocean was cloudy — from the dynamite."

Kaz shook his head. "Scientists don't destroy coral. They *love* coral. Every day is like take-a-polyp-to-lunch day."

"That's exactly why we've been having so much trouble trying to figure this thing out," Star told him. "Why would a scientist steal our coin? Why would a scientist waste our time tagging caves? The answer is: Cutter, Marina, and Reardon aren't scientists. They're treasure hunters."

"Treasure hunters!" Kaz exclaimed. "It all adds up. They sure aren't oceanographers. Did you catch what Cutter said over the radio? 'Was that a whale?'"

Dante was skeptical. "But if treasure's what they're really after, why would they bring in four kids on summer internships? Wouldn't we just be in the way?"

"I think we're kind of a smoke screen," Adriana put in. "Remember, Cutter's people don't work at Poseidon, Saint-Luc. They're from the head office in California. It's the perfect cover —

they come here and nose around the Hidden Shoals, acting like it's for our benefit."

"And they keep us out of their hair," Star added, "by sending us after caves nobody cares about."

Kaz nodded slowly. "And they picked *us* because we wouldn't be good enough to interfere with their discovery."

"If they make a discovery," Dante added.

"They already did," said Adriana. "Or at least, you did."

Wordlessly, Star reached into the pocket of her cargo shorts and drew out the artifact she had pulled from the wreckage of the coral — the carved white handle. "The anchor, the silver coin, and now this, all in the same spot. Are you going to tell me there isn't a wreck down there?"

The two boys' eyes widened as they stared at the gleaming whalebone hilt. A pockmark of coral growth obscured its main decoration — a large dark stone inset in the delicate pattern. Directly above it were etched the initials JB. The old English script was as sharp as if it had been carved only yesterday.

JB. Was that some poor shipwrecked sailor, dead for hundreds of years?

28 August 1665

The cruel crack of Captain James Blade's whip was familiar now. The percussive snap of oiled leather slicing into lacerated skin, the agonized howls of the unfortunate seaman, the evil green flash of the huge emerald embedded in the handle of the captain's favorite implement of torture.

Today's victim was Clark, the bosun's mate. But in the man's piteous complaint, young Samuel Higgins could hear the cries of Evans the sail maker, the only person on this earth who had ever befriended an orphaned cabin boy. Old Evans, now long dead, like so many others on this terrible crossing.

The captain was rearing back for another brutal lash when the shout was heard from the rigging.

"Land, ho!"

And, mercifully, the flogging was over. The celebration was unlike anything Samuel had ever seen — a mad scramble for the gunwales, all eyes straining to drink in the narrow green-brown ribbon barely visible on the horizon. After four long months at sea, suffering harsh treatment and privations, watching more than half of their numbers succumb to malnutrition, fever, and scurvy, the weary crew of the Griffin had reached the New World. On a boat with a stench fouler than the filthiest sewer in Liverpool, the tattered seamen danced and cheered like children on May Day.

The captain peered through his long spyglass and emitted a bellow of triumph. "Portobelo, by God! Just a few miles down the coast!" There was a roar of approval from the assembled throng.

York reached out a dirty hand and ruffled Samuel's unruly hair. "To traverse the great sea and strike land a cannon shot from your destination! Aye, boy, that's like firing a musket ball half a league straight through a keyhole! You're a lucky one, Samuel Higgins. Well named, you are."

Praise from the ghoulish barber always made Samuel's skin crawl. But the feeling quickly dissipated, swept up in the joy of their arrival. Land! The endless voyage was finally over.

He ran his fingers through the few copper coins in his breeches — meager wages for these long months at sea, yet still more money than he had ever held in his thirteen years. "Clean water," he said aloud. "That's what I'll ask for first. And bread — fresh baked, with no maggots in it."

"Are you feebleminded, boy?" York cried in disbelief. "That little town there is the western terminus of the Spanish treasure fleet, the richest place in all Creation. We're not here to visit, Lucky. We're here to plunder their treasure and burn their city to the ground!"